TO THE SHORES OF TRIPOLI

A Battlestreamers of the Marine Corps Book

By Colonel Jonathan P. Brazee, USMCR (Ret)

Semper Fi Press
Copyright © 2013 Jonathan P. Brazee

A Semper Fi Press Book

- ISBN-10: 0615777201
- ISBN-13: 978-0615777207

Printed in the United States of America

This is a work of historical fiction. The three protagonists and most of the dialogue are products of the author's imagination and are used fictitiously. Other characters, actions taken, and some dialogue are taken from existing historical records.

Acknowledgements:

This book was a labor of love, but I could not have finished it without the tremendous assistance given to me by the US Marine Corps History Division, especially that of Annette Amerman, Colonel Peter Ferraro, and most of all, that of Owen Conner. Their help in locating documents pertaining to the war, uniforms, weapons, and the history of the mameluke sword were vital in making this book historically accurate. From VFW Post 9951 in Bangkok, I need to thank Ricky Reece, MacAlan Thompson, and Bill Bernstrom for their proofreading and fact-checking. Suellen May and Ann Bunch were invaluable in their proofreading. And I need to thank my editor, Beth Bruno, for all her hard work to keep me on the straight and narrow in order to write the best possible book I could. The assistance I received in writing this book was invaluable. All remaining mistakes and inaccuracies are solely my fault.

Cover Art: *Attack on Derna,*
by Colonel Charles Waterhouse, USMCR (Ret)
Public Domain

Cover Design by Jonathan Brazee

Additional Proofreading by Gabrielle West

Dedicated to the Marines who lost their lives in the First Barbary War:

Sergeant Jonathan Meridith
Private William Williams
Private Nathaniel Holmes
Private John Whitten
Private Edward Steward

RIP

Author's Note

This novel was a work of love, but it was also very difficult and time-consuming to research. The First Barbary War was not well-documented, and what was written about it was often at odds with other writings. Even what was an accepted truth at one time proved to be inaccurate later. One example is that of Able Seaman Reuben James. As a midshipman at the Naval Academy, I was taught that James saved the life of Stephen Decatur during the Gunboat Battle by interposing himself between the lieutenant and a descending Tripolitan blade, taking the blow to the head. The US Navy has even named three ships after him. However, further research shows that no one by the name of James received any medical treatment after the battle. A Daniel Frazier, on the other hand, was treated for a saber slash to the head, and he was a member of Decatur's boarding party. There were a few mentions in various texts of Frazier as the one who saved Decatur, but it was James who received the credit until very recently.

Given the differing versions of written history on the war, I had to choose one version over the other in my own story. An example of this was when one member of the crew of the *Philadelphia* received a *bastinado*, a type of punishment, for beating another American while they were prisoners of the Tripolitans. Some accounts had it that the person beaten was John Wilson, a "turk," that is, a crew member who turned to Islam in order to escape the condition of slavery. Other accounts have it that the person beaten was a warrant officer, and John Wilson used his position to settle an old score and have a Marine sergeant given the *bastinado*. I took the license in having the person given the punishment being one of my three fictional protagonists.

I chose to have three fictional characters as my literary points of view. None of the three have any basis in history. Almost every other character, on the other hand, was an actual historical figure. I was able to research the personalities and even actual dialogue of many of the major historical characters, but for others, only their names were recorded. Of the Marines who fought in the Battle of Derne, for example, the only thing known of the enlisted men, other than who was killed and who was wounded, was that sometimes Private John Whitten danced the jig while Lieutenant O'Bannon played the fiddle. Consequently, all characterizations of many of the actual historical figures in the book come entirely from my imagination.

One small happy coincidence is that accounts of the Battle of Derne relate that the Marines consisted of Lieutenant O'Bannon and an acting sergeant and either six or seven privates, but only the names of five privates were ever recorded. That left a spot for Private Jacob Brissey, one of my fictional protagonists.

I made liberal use of direct quotes and historical documents throughout the book. Some of those documents used spelling and punctuation that was neither uniform nor in keeping with modern English usage. Initially, I quoted those documents verbatim, but both my editor as well as my pre-publication readers recommended that I correct at least some of the more egregious permutations.

Finally, I had to make a decision as to the dialogue of my characters. I could "modern up" the language used, to make it flow better for present-day readers. Instead, I chose to use the period language of the time. I read a number of period pieces, complete with dialogue, to create the voice of Jacob Brissey in particular. For Ichabod Cone and Seth Crocker, I relied more on period dictionaries of slang, or the "vulgar tongue," as it was often termed. I have included a glossary at the end of the novel of many of the terms I used. I hope I was able to present an accurate voice for the book, yet still keep it easily digestible by readers.

MAP OF THE BARBARY STATES

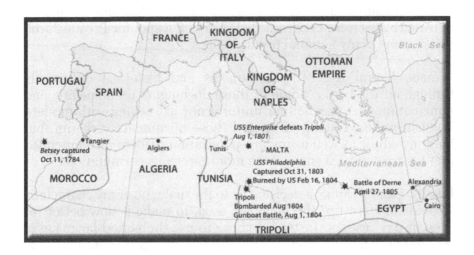

Oct 11, 1784
100 Miles off the coast of Africa

Captain James Erwin took the spyglass from his first mate and focused in on the British corvette flying the Guinea Jack that identified it as a ship of the Royal African Company. It was closing in from the port quarter, and even a year before, this would have been cause for alarm. Until the signing of the Treaty of Paris almost 13 months earlier, Britain still considered the United States as part of its empire, and sailors were often taken from American merchantmen and impressed into the Royal Navy. Captain Erwin felt a twinge of concern, but not enough to try and outrun the corvette. The British captain probably wanted to give or receive information about sea conditions.

The *Betsey* was a 350-ton brigantine out of Baltimore with a load of salt from Cadiz, bound for Philadelphia. She was a quick, nimble ship with a crew of 10, and her initial crossing had been uneventful. The captain looked forward to returning to the United States, offloading, then taking in new cargo for another run.

"Orders, captain?" his first mate asked.

"Keep her steady. Let's see what they want," he replied.

John Harris, the first mate, merely shrugged. He'd spent two years impressed into the Royal Navy, and it was all the same to him.

The corvette slowly moved closer. Only the helmsman, a few deck hands, and a ship's officer, resplendent in his company uniform, were visible on deck. The officer had moved to the starboard rail and looked to hail the *Betsey*.

"Where are you out of?" he shouted when the two ships were about 40 yards apart.

"This is the *Betsey*, out of Baltimore, bound for Philadelphia," the captain shouted back.

"If that is so, then prepare to be boarded!" the officer yelled across the water.

The captain's heart fell as he turned to give the helmsman the order to come about in an attempt to put distance between the two ships.

The British corvette's five starboard gun ports opened, and one gun fired a shot across the *Betsey*'s bow before the ship could move. The Guinea Jack came down and was replaced by an ensign that the captain didn't recognize.

The captain hesitated a moment, calculating his chances. The *Betsey* had no guns, but like all ships she had small arms aboard.

"Mr. Harris, get all hands on deck, then break out the muskets, but don't fire unless I give the order," he told his first mate.

He moved over to the rail, wondering what he could do to give his ship more time. He was about to issue new orders when from below the starboard rail of the corvette, at least 50 turbaned, shirtless men jumped up from where they had been hidden. All were armed with pistols and swords and started to shout at the top of their lungs.

Captain Erwin was no fool. He knew the *Betsey* had no chance. When the first grappling hooks came flying over, he stopped one seaman from cutting the hook free. These were either Tripolitans or Algerines, and now that American ships were no longer under the protection of the British Navy, it wasn't surprising that they were considered fair game.

"Leave it be, Alfred," he told the young seaman.

The two ships were brought together, and despite his intention to go quietly, he still felt a rush of anger when the first of the pirates surged aboard. How dare they do this to his ship, his first command?

The supposed British officer had shed his tunic and roundabout before boarding. He spotted the captain and strode up to him, surrounded by his men. Just then, however, Mr. Harris appeared from below decks, three muskets cradled in his arms.

With a bellow, one huge Mahomaten rushed the confused first mate, and with one swing of his curved sword, struck the poor man down, completely severing his arm and shoulder. Mr. Harris fell without a cry, blood pouring out on the deck.

Two of his sailors cried out and started to move forward, but the captain stepped in front of them, stopping them from doing anything foolish. He should have stopped the first mate from coming out armed, but what was done was done.

The pirate leader sneered at the dying first mate. He nodded at the big pirate who had struck the blow, who then stepped back, glaring as if daring someone else to make a move.

The leader turned back to the captain, and in a voice loud enough for the entire crew to hear, shouted, "Christian dogs, you are now slaves of Mohammed Ben Abdellah al-Khath of the Sultanate of Morocco!"

1801

Three months after the seizure of the *Betsey*, the ship and crew were released after Spain had interceded with promises that the new American government would negotiate treaties with the four Barbary States. Thomas Jefferson, the minister to France, sent envoys to Morocco and Algeria in order to purchase treaties. On June 21, 1786, the Sultan of Morocco signed a treaty guaranteeing the safety of all American ships and citizens.

Algerian pirates had seized the *Maria* on July 25, 1785 and the *Dauphin* a week later. The American envoys sent to Algeria had a budget of $40,000 to secure the release of the crews, but the Algerians demanded $660,000. No treaty was signed until 10 years later when the United States paid more than $1,000,000 in ransom for the 115 citizens being held as slaves, an amount that represented 1/6 of the total U.S. budget at the time.

Efforts to resolve the hostage situation with Tripoli did not fare much better. During March of 1785, Thomas Jefferson and John Adams traveled to London in an attempt to negotiate a treaty with Tripoli's envoy, Ambassador Sidi Haji Abdrahaman. When they inquired, "concerning the ground of the pretensions to make war upon nations who had done them no injury," the ambassador replied, as later relayed by Jefferson to the Secretary of Foreign Affairs, John Jay:

It was written in their Koran, that all nations which had not acknowledged the Prophet were sinners, whom it was the right and duty of the faithful to plunder and enslave; and that every mussulman who was slain in this warfare was sure to go to paradise. He said, also, that the man who was the first to board a vessel had one slave over and above his share, and that when they sprang to the deck of an enemy's ship, every sailor held a dagger in each hand and a third in his mouth; which usually struck such terror into the foe that they cried out for quarter at once.

Jefferson argued that paying such a ransom would only further encourage the Barbary States to seize American vessels, and President Adams agreed, but without a navy, Adams felt the payments had to be made, and the yearly tribute of $1 million was authorized.

In 1798, the US Navy and Marines were formed to provide protection for U.S. shipping. In 1801, just prior to Jefferson's inauguration, six frigates were authorized to "be officered and manned as the President of the United States may direct," wording that has had long-term consequences in the history of the country with regards to war powers. In the event of a declaration of war on the United States by the Barbary powers, these ships were to "protect our commerce & chastise their insolence — by sinking, burning or destroying their ships & Vessels wherever you shall find them."

By the time of Jefferson's inauguration, the United States was paying Tripoli $46,000 a year in protection money. Yusuf Karamanli, the Pasha of Tripoli, sought to increase that to $250,000. Jefferson, in keeping with his principles, refused. The Pasha declared war on the United States by cutting down the flagpole at the U.S. consulate.

The United States was at war.

Jonathan P. Brazee

Chapter 1

Philadelphia
March, 1801

Jacob

I looked at the bill I had taken the night before. This was the place, but it didn't look like a recruiting station. It was an alehouse. Across the street, though, was the entrance to the Navy Yard, and the name of the place was correct, so I stepped in, eyes adjusting to the dark. The sour-hoppy smell of ale was enticing, but I sure couldn't afford a drink, so I ignored my thirst and stepped up to the bar to ask instead of ordering.

"Is this where I can enlist in the Marines?" I asked the barkeep as he looked up at me.

The fat man merely hooked his thumb towards a table to the right where two other men sat. I walked over, not certain what to say, and the older of the two men kicked out a chair for me to take a seat.

"Are you Marines?" I asked. Neither man was in uniform.

"Nah, not yet. Don' really wanna be either, God's truth," the younger of the two offered up. "We're waiting for the sergeant to shows up and sign us up."

I sat down, opening up my coat a bit. It was pretty threadbare, not enough to keep me warm in the February morning, but inside the alehouse, a fire kept things pretty warm.

"What do you mean? If you don't want to be a Marine, why're you here?"

"'Cause the Navy's already hit their numbers," he told me. "So I comes here instead."

Navy or Marines, I really didn't care. I thought they were the same, to be honest. All I cared about was getting a job. The bill promised a steady job, and my belly was rubbing against my backbone. But his comments had me curious.

"Why's the Navy any better?"

"Two dollars," the older man answered while the younger fellow nodded.

Neither seemed inclined to extrapolate any further, so I asked, "Two dollars? What do you mean?"

"Seamen get $12 a month. Marines get $10 a month. Just last year, privates got only $6 a month, so this is a jump 'im up," the older man said. "Seamen only enlist for one year, but Marines enlist for three, so you need to keep that in mind before you muster up."

That took me aback. Why was there a difference? I didn't even know the difference between a seaman and a Marine. Three years ago, I wouldn't have cared. But when yellow fever hit the flats of New York, taking Suva's parents, I lost my future as a tradesman. I was supposed to take over Suva's father's cooper shop after we married, but with no family of my own, and now with Suva an orphan as well, that rosy future fell by the wayside. Now, three years later, I was willing to take whatever job came along.

But maybe I should know just what I was getting myself into.

"So what is a Marine actually?" I asked, leaving the question broad.

Instead of answering, the older man held out his hand.

"Ichabod Cone," he said in introduction.

"Jacob Brissey," I answered. "Pleased to make your acquaintance."

"Seth Crocker," the younger man said, his hand out as well.

Ichabod motioned to the barkeep for a round, pointing at me, holding up a few coins. I wanted to protest, but it had been awhile since I had had a drink.

"Thanks…" I started, but he waved me off.

"As to what is a Marine? Well, the dogs of a ship, second class-citizens. We man the tops in a fight, we repel borders, we lead landing parties. But we are second-class citizens, make no doubt about it. What we aren't are tars. We're not seamen, and we don't sail ships."

"I suppose I'm still confused. Why doesn't the Army do that?"

Ichabod laughed, then added, "No soldier worth his salt'll get on a ship. We like mother earth, thankee much."

"We?" Seth and I asked in unison.

"I served with Washington himself in the Continental Army." He rolled up one sleeve to show a huge gouge that scarred his arm. "Got this

7

at Brandywine. Got another, even bigger, at Monmouth, thanks to the British cannonade. Can't show you that, though."

"Why not?" I asked, fascinated by the tortured flesh of his arm.

"'Cause it's on my bumfiddle[1] there, lad. Can't very well strip down naked here, right?"

"So why not join the Army?" I asked him.

"I was at Valley Forge, too, and never was I so hungry in my life. At least ships carry food, so I thought I'd give this a try." He paused for a moment , then with a shrug and a smile, continued. "Well, that and the fact that I can't get in the Army now no neverhow, what with them disbanding."

Ichabod was rail thin. His hair, what there was of it, was turning gray. It looked like he had missed more than a meal or two in his life, so if he had been at Valley Forge, he must have looked like a scarecrow.

I looked over at Seth. What Ichabod might have lacked in bulk, Seth more than made up for. He was short, but his shoulders were broad, hinting at a life of hard labor. His hair was blonde, but it might have been a long time since it had seen soap or water. His eyes were a pale blue, looking soft and feminine, which belied his brawler's frame.

"So if you don't know what a Marine is, why're you here?" Ichabod asked.

I didn't know how much I wanted to tell them. I wasn't proud of not being able to make a living. No man was. But I didn't want to lie.

"I came here from New York after yellow fever took my fiancée's family. She survived but came to Princeton to live with her aunt while I'm trying to earn enough to marry her and start a family. I've been stevedoring, but there's not much to be made, and with the French troubles, not enough work. So when I saw the bill posted on a wall, I thought this might be an answer."

"You came from New York because of yellow fever? Here, to Philadelphia, the yellow fever center of the country?" Ichabod asked. "You talk like an educated man, so didn't you know about the fever the Santa Domingans brought? I know there were Philadelphia refugees going to New York. We read about your mayor rushing to protect your nanny houses[2] from our erstwhile brothers."

---

[1] Bumfiddle: the buttocks

I had to laugh. Our esteemed Mayor Varick couldn't give a flick about the flats, but let the lower classes threaten the brothels, then he was there at the front lines of defense. He'd been the talk of the town at the time, none of it complimentary.

"I knew your mayor when he was General Washington's secretary, and he always pissed more than he drank back then, too."

"Yeah, that's one way to put it," I said. "Pissed more than he drank" was an apt description of the vainglorious man.

I looked over at Seth who was quietly sipping his mug of beer. He looked like a brawler, but his face was smooth, nary a hair on his chin.

"What about you?" I asked him. "Why're you signing up?"

"Not much to say. My pa's farm failed, and my older brother's got claim to it anyhoo. Too many mouths to feed, so I has to go find my own way. I came for the Navy, but they's all full up, so the Marine Corps'll do for me."

I looked at him closer. He had the bulk of a man, but his face was young.

"How old are you?" I had to ask.

"Sixteen, thereabouts," he replied, taking another sip from his mug.

Ichabod perked up at that and took a closer look at our companion.

"You're 16?" he asked.

"Like I said, thereabouts."

"No, you're 18," Ichabod told him.

"I may not be educated no how, but I thinks I know how old I am."

"No, you're 18 if you want to enlist today. They don't take privates under 18."

I hadn't known that. I don't think I ever even thought about it before. I looked over at Seth, who merely shrugged.

"Did I says 16? No, I means 18," he said calmly, taking yet one more sip.

Ichabod laughed, motioning to the barkeep for another round. "You're going to do well, young man. You're going to fit right in."

Just then, a man in uniform came into the tavern, blinking as his eyes adjusted. He looked over at the barkeep, who tilted his head in our direction. The man was dressed in a dark blue uniform with red facings, a

---

[2] Nanny house: house of prostitution

white roundabout and pants with white leggings. His broad face was almost pink, and his red hair was tied behind his head. This was a Marine, I presumed.

"Only three?" he asked no one in particular as he looked us over. "Any of you got military experience?"

"I served with General Washington," Ichabod responded.

The Marine's eyebrows arched, and he nodded in what seemed to be grudging respect. "That'll do. We've gotten Legion soldiers lately, but not many from the War. After we sign the papers, you're in charge. I'm Sergeant Morris, and I'm going to be mustering you in."

He pulled his haversack around in front of him and reached for some papers. He didn't ask if we had any questions but acted on the presumption that everything was already decided. I guess I didn't have much choice, but I think I would have liked at least the pretense that this was what I wanted, lack of a job be damned.

He took out three documents, a pen and ink, a ledger, and sat down.

"Name, age and place of birth?" he asked Ichabod, writing the name on the document, then the rest in a ledger. He noted Ichabod's height and weight, then wrote down a description of the scar on his arm. He asked him to sign the muster papers, making them official.

He asked me next, then Seth. He didn't hesitate when Seth boldly told him he was 18 years old. Seth surprised me when he told the sergeant that he couldn't sign his name. Unfazed, the sergeant wrote it in and asked Seth to mark the signature. After blowing a bit on the documents to dry the ink, he stood up.

"Private Cone, I want you to take these two and follow me. The important part's done, but first you need a physical examination, then the lieutenant's going to give you your oath tomorrow. You'll get $2 each as an advance and $2 for expenses, and then you'll be off to Washington for your uniforms, training, and assignment. Until you arrive, Cone, you're in command."

I started for a moment. Washington? The new capital?

"Uh, sergeant, sir, I thought the Marines were based here in Philadelphia," I said.

He looked at me and laughed. "We moved to Washington last month, lad. To our brand-new barracks."

Washington? That was a long way from Princeton. How would I be able to see Suva?

"Sergeant, I joined because I thought I would be here in Philadelphia."

His sense of humor seemed to vanish. "Doesn't matter much nohow, does it? You're going to be on a ship soon, and not here in Philadelphia or Washington. 'Sides, I got your signature here, so you ain't got much choice. Now then, Private Cone, you've got your orders. Get these two and follow me for your oath."

I realized that even without my signature, I didn't have much choice. With a sigh, and wondering what I had gotten myself into, I stood up and followed Ichabod out of the alehouse.

Chapter 2

Washington DC
April

Ichabod

"God's mercy, Ichabod, I keeps forgetting which one's the right and which one's the left. I thinks I gots them mixed up again," Seth groaned, pulling off his ankle boot and wool sock and rubbing his foot.

"I told you to mark one as the right so you don't get them confused," I told him for about the hundredth time.

"I knows, I knows, but I keeps forgetting."

I had initially taken Seth to be nothing more than a country bumpkin, but he had shown me that he wasn't a nick ninny. But in this, his forgetfulness had a price to pay. He had two huge open blisters on his foot. Not that any of the rest of us had it much better. My boots, though, were already starting to take shape as one for my right foot, one for my left. But then again, I had marked the sole of one with an "X," and that one always went onto my right foot. With Seth, if he kept switching them around, they were never going to conform to each foot.

We had been issued our uniforms when we arrived at the new barracks. The white roundabout shirt and vest were fairly standard, and the linen underclothes were actually quite nice. The boots were somewhat low quality, but at least we were shod. At Valley Forge, I had to bind my feet with blankets, so anything was better than that.

I wasn't as happy with the pantaloons, though. For me, they were too tight, and if I was going to be climbing like an African monkey in the tops at my age, I wanted freedom of movement. I think breeches are more comfortable, but the sergeant quartermaster said something about going away from French styles due to the recent bad feelings between our two countries. With the gaiters tight around my calves, I felt like my legs were too restricted.

Our coats, however, were leftovers from Mad Anthony Wayne's legion, blue with red facings. I had expected the Marines to have something in line with their Continental Marine forerunners, but these were just Legion hand-me-downs.

I was rather taken with our hats. These were the new rounds, as they called them, each one with a bear crest ridge. I thought they looked rather smart.

We were meant to receive two pair of woolen and two pair of linen overalls for our dirty work, but we received only one pair of the linen ones. Likewise, we received only one pair of shoes. Jacob asked when we would receive the rest, but the sergeant quartermaster had no answer. He told us that recruits going directly to ships in New York and Boston had even less of their kit.

Even so, with the socks, the other three shirts, the blanket, and the stock and clasp, we were well clad. Seth mentioned that he had never had so much to wear in his life.

"Hey, get those back on," Jacob told Seth. "Here comes the sergeant."

We had just marched from the temporary barracks to the Navy Yard, and we were finally going to fire our muskets. For the last week, we had been drilling back in the barracks with wooden sticks, like little boys playing soldier. Over and over again, we went through the commands until they were ingrained in our heads. Even the dimmest of us had it down.

Behind the approaching sergeant were two privates pulling a handcart. On the handcart were ten muskets. I was surprised, though, to see the same Charlevilles I had used in the war. I knew our armory in Springfield had been making an improved version of the musket for over six years, but these were definitely old war stock. I could tell by the shape of the flash pan. I was disappointed, but at least I was familiar with the weapon. It was only a .69 caliber, unlike the British Brown Bess at .75 caliber, but .69 was plenty big enough to do damage, and we could carry more balls in our tin.

Sergeant Lafarge had a deep, gravelly voice, and he went over the commands yet again before we were told to line up and take a musket. I was in the first group, and when the Charleville was handed to me, I felt transported back to my first one in the war. It felt familiar in my hands.

This one had seen some wear, but it looked to be in good condition. It had a new flint, was well-oiled, and had no major signs of damage. I wish I could say I had aged as well myself over the last 20 years or so.

We were told to line up at the small range at the river's edge, and then one of the privates came down the line, handing us one ball each, while the other private handed us a cartridge of powder. I guess they didn't trust us yet with more than one shot apiece.

Downrange, at about 25 yards away, were several tree stumps set upright; a clay crock sat on one of them. Accuracy didn't seem to be an issue at this stage of training. Procedures would be king today.

The sergeant ordered us to attention before beginning his commands. He checked each Marine to make sure his musket was at half-cock. Some Marines, like Jacob, had never fired a weapon before, and it was easy for the musket to fire before the shooter was ready. Half-cock prevented accidental firing.

His loud order of "load arms" snapped me to, and hours of repetition took over. On "open pans," my hand went right to the frizzen, the lid over the pan, and opened it. Some men liked to put the shot into the barrel first, but the military was the military, and we were expected to prepare the pan before loading the shot.

"Handle cartridge" and "tear cartridge" came next with teeth tearing open the paper so the powder could be poured out. At "prime," I poured a small amount into the pan, giving something for the flint to ignite. At "close pans," the frizzen was flipped, sealing in the powder.

The sergeant was taking it slow. In battle a soldier had to fire three rounds in a minute. Here, we had already passed a minute, and we still hadn't begun to load the shot.

The sergeant walked up and down the line, inspecting each step. He had to assist several privates, Jacob included, in getting the right amount of powder into the pans, and now he was inspecting each musket before proceeding. He barely glanced at mine, though, and I have to admit that gave me a surge of pride.

At "load," the butt of the musket was placed on the ground. "Cartridge into the barrel" came next, and the lead shot, which was wrapped in a piece of paper, was dropped into place. "Draw ramrod" and "ram down cartridge" followed, and I took the iron ramrod and drove the shot home. My first Charleville had a wooden ramrod, so this was an improvement.

The sergeant bellowed out "return ramrod," "shoulder arms," "make ready." After all that work, we were finally ready to fire. At "present," we aimed at the wooden stumps. I drew on the clay crock. I wanted to see it shatter. At "fire," a volley of 10 shots rang out and black smoke billowed out to surround us. It took a few moments for it to clear, and while there were several gouges in two of the stumps, the crock was still standing whole. I wasn't too surprised. A musket was accurate to about 50 or 75 yards, but after that, the shots tended to go their own way. Until we could get a feel for our individual weapon, even shorter shots could be difficult.

We fired five rounds before giving up our weapons to the next 10 privates. I went back to the rear and sat down, then brought out the bread and dried beef that made up my lunch from my haversack. The smell of the black powder brought me back even more than the firing orders. And as I took a bite of bread, the familiar tang of the powder, which had gotten into my mouth as I bit open the cartridges, reminded me of battles long past.

Seth flopped down beside me, pulling out his lunch as well. Jacob, though, had his canteen out and was trying to wash the black powder from his mouth. I just smiled. He would learn that water was too valuable to waste on that. He'd learn to eat with the sweet spice of powder flavoring whatever food he could get.

"That was easy," Seth said as he took a bite of his bread.

"Easy here, yes. But try it when you've got a line of redcoats across the meadow, all firing at you. Tightens up the old feak, I tell you."

Jacob finally sat down to join us. The three of us had formed a bond, starting up in Philadelphia, which had only strengthened during our time at the barracks. There were other good lads there, too, but the three of us were a team.

"Well, maybe so," Seth said. "But I says we need good Pennsylvania long rifles. Can't hit nothin' with these smoothbores. With my pa's rifle, I can shave a squirrel's whiskers at half-a-mile."

"Rifles are good, but massed fire is what wins battles. You can't fire but one round every minute-and-a-half with a rifle, and after four or five shots, the barrel's fouled."

"Yeah, but I can hit what I wants with a rifle," he persisted.

I felt what I figured was a fatherly affection for the young farmboy. I never had kids, so I couldn't be sure, but he tickled my fancy at times. He was so earnest, so sure of himself.

"So when that line of lobsterbacks charges you, bayonets at the ready, which one of those hundred men are you going to take out with that rifle before they reach you and turn you into a pincushion?"

"Well, we're not fighting redcoats, are we? We're going out to fight Mahomaten pirates," he harrumphed.

I let him be, knowing he got my point.

We sat back for the next two hours as the others fired. Taking every opportunity to do nothing was a time-honored tradition of soldiers going back to the Romans, and if it worked for them, why should we change anything? Finally, though, we were told to march along the river to the first dock where a small ship of some sort was tied up. I 'spect I would learn more about all the ships, but for now, I couldn't tell one ship from another.

This ship had two masts, and there were ladders running up each mast to a small wooden platform about a third of the way up it. Sergeant Lafarge told us that we were going to fire from those.

Firing from solid ground was something I was used to. Climbing that rope ladder and firing from up there was something else. Suddenly, I was not too sure of myself.

Of course, Sergeant Lafarge called me out to be one of the first four men to fire, two to each mast. I noted that all four of us had served before, in either a militia, a legion, or in the Army.

We walked over a rickety gangway and onto the ship. We were in the Potomac River, not the ocean, but still, the ship rocked slightly back and forth. I looked up the ladder with more than a bit of dread.

Each musket had a white buffalo-hide sling, so it went onto my back as I grasped the ladder and started on my way up. The ladder swayed back and forth, and several times I had to hug it tight to keep from falling. Somehow, I made it to the platform and eagerly clambered on.

Along with Private Simms, who had been in the Virginia Militia and was one of the more experienced privates to oversee us, it was crowded. I tried not to look down.

With his accent, which made what he said a little hard to understand at times, Sergeant Lafarge bellowed from below to look into the water. It was only then that I noticed a large wooden crate, floating just off the side of the ship. The river tried to sweep it away, but it was securely tied in place, maybe to a large rock or anchor. This was to be our target.

Sergeant Lafarge went through the firing orders once more. What was easy on land was not so easy perched up in the air like some bird. I kept bumping into Simms and he into me, but eventually we were ready. When the order came to fire, all four of us on the ship opened up. To my surprise, my own shot joined the others as too long. None of us hit the crate, and I had overshot it by several feet. Unfamiliar musket or not, I should have been able to hit it.

After four shots apiece, the crate had been hit exactly twice and not once by me, to my shame. I clambered down the ladder and handed over the musket to the next private, then went to sit down.

"You needs to aim lower," Seth said as he came up to where I was sitting.

I looked up at him, not wanting any advice from a 16-year-old child.

"I says you needs to aim lower."

"Why?" I asked, curious despite myself.

"What you calls it, 'gravity?' When you shoot from the ground into a tree, you needs to aim lower, too, 'cause gravity doesn't suck so much on your shot."

"What?" I asked, pretty confused.

"I can't says it good, but when you is higher or lower than your target, you have to aim different than if you is both on the same level."

"Ah, I understand," Jacob said. "Yes, gravity won't affect your trajectory as much the more vertical the shot, vertical up or down. So if you aim as if you were on the level ground, gravity won't have a chance to pull your ball as much. So you have to aim lower, as Seth says, to hit the target."

I was still a mite confused, but with Jacob using his hands to demonstrate what he was saying, I began to catch their drift. Next time, I would do better. And I would have many more chances to do it. The rumor was that the Navy was soon to ship out, and we would be getting posted soon, but until then, if I knew anything about the military, free time would be a luxury, and practice, practice, practice would be our way of life.

Chapter 3

Washington DC
April 3, 1801

Seth

"Huzzah!" we all shouts after the commandant speaks to us.

I don' listen to all of what he says, but it's be brave, fight hard, things like that. Lieutenant Colonel Burrows ain't neither a cock robin or a turk, but just a real nib.[3] And he speaks like a nib, all educated and proper-like. I just let my mind goes free when he's talking at us. We all already knows that's the Secretary of the Navy's tells him the day 'fore yesterday that he has to gets 50 Marines on the Navy's four frigates and 30 on the schooner *Enterprise* to go fight the Mahomaten.

Standing next to me is Jacob. It's hard to believe that he's like my brother now, more than my real brothers. He's a right good cull. Last night, once again, he offers to write my folks, and when I says no, I can sees it bothers him. Him being an orphan twice now, what with his blood kin dying when he's a lad, then his second father, his Suva's pa, he keeps saying to me that I'm lucky to have a family. What he don' knows is that I would rather be him, with my family taken by God's hand rather than having them turn me out like they did.

Now, he's part of my new family, like the rest of the Marines aside me. Him and Ichabod are the closest, but all of them, 'cepting maybe that hog-grubber Dickson, they're my new brothers.

The commandant marches off with the rest of the officers, then Sergeant Major Sommers tells us to go back to the barracks and get ready to leave. The sergeant major might look like a nib, too, all polished like in his uniform, but he's a real hackum. I wrestles him once, and he trounces

---

[3] Nib: a proper gentleman

me. I like him. He may have that new rank, the first one to get it, but I thinks he could be just as happy as a private like the rest of us.

The drummers and fifers plays as we breaks our parade. I likes their uniform, and even their dollar a month they makes more than us, but I wants to fight, not plays music.

Ichabod needs to hurry. A wagon's taking him and the others to Baltimore to board the *Philadelphia*, the Navy's newest frigate. Jacob, he's going to the *United States*, another big frigate. Me, I'm going to the *Enterprise*, the schooner. I donst know just what a schooner is yet, but I reckons I'll find out soon enough. We donst have 30 Marines neither, only eight privates, one sergeant, and a lieutenant. But my ships, she's not even gots her masts on yet, so we won't sail until next month. Ichabod and Jacob, though, they need to join their ships now.

Just a year or two afore, most Marines, they goes to the ships that the ship's lieutenant of Marines recruits them for. But with the new Marines, our commandant, he sends our "rendezvous stations," he calls them, then has all of us recruits trained together like, and he decides where most of us goes. I wishes, though, that for this, we was under the old ways, and us three would go together on the *Philadelphia*.

I looks around as everyone scurries like ants at a fire, rushing to get ready. I can hear the horses snorting outside the gates, ready to take the wagons north. I has only been here a month, but I feels like I belong.

I turns and walks back to the barracks, shouldering my Brown Bess. I got lucky with that. After I wrestled the sergeant major, he asks me about training, and I tells him I don' like the Charleville. He gets me a Brown Bess, like the redcoats use. Ichabod, he likes the Charlevilles, says he can carry more shot. But that's for the Army. On a ship, she carries the shot for us. The Brown Bess has a shorter barrel, and iffen I have to shoot with all the ratlines, Jacob's ladders, shrouds, jibs, and all those other Navy riggings, then I think a shorter barrel mightn't gets caught up like the longer one. And the sergeant major, he tells me that the Brown Bess is easier to take care of on a ship.

Ichabod thinks he knows everything 'cause he fought with Washington, and he's smart. I looks down at the small notch on the sole of my right shoe and smile. He did that, and now my shoes are not torture every time I put them on. But he don' knows everything.

I stands outside the door to the barracks and wait until Ichabod comes out. He stops to shake my hand, but I hug him instead.

"Take care, lad," he says. "Let's meet up in Gibraltar for a beer."

I wish we were all together to fight the Mahomatens, but we has to accepts it.

"I'll hold you to that," I tells him, trying not to let a tear roll down my cheek.

Jacob comes out, ready to go, too. His wagons will leave next, but he's got a few minutes. I hug him too. I'm going to miss him. I never thought I could get well with an educated man like him, but he teaches me about history, about science, never talking down to me. I never even knew what a Mahomaten was until he told me about Muhammed and the Arabs. Nows I do. I knows good Christian folks, even if they was British and French, been fighting the Mahomatens for years, in what they calls the Crusades.

He pushes a piece of paper in my hands. I looks down at it. It's got writing on it. Jacob's been showing me the letters, and I can even write my name now, but as for real writing, I'm guessing I do all right as I is.

"Practice these, like I've shown you," he whispers in my ear before I lets him out of my hug.

The sergeants are yelling loud as coon hounds for everyone to get on the wagons. My two friends hesitate a moment.

Here we are. An old War of Independence soldier, who we still donst know why he joined up. An educated man from New York. And a Pennsylvania farm boy. Each of us is different, but each of us is now the same. We're Marines now. In the old days, I hears they just conscript you, and you go on the ship that day. I thinks our training here brings us together, makes us part of a team.

It's time, though. Ichabod has to leave.

He steps back and wishes us "fair winds and following seas, lads."

Then he's gone. Training is over, and now the real adventure begins

Chapter 4

The USS Enterprise
August 1

Seth

I was at the ship's bow, as was my wont in the morning, taking in the breeze after spending the night in my hammock in the foul berthing spaces. Life was good aboard the ship. Lieutenant Sterett, our captain, a hard man but a real gentleman, treats even the Marines as worthy men. Our Marine commander, 2nd Lieutenant Enoch Lane, was a swell,[4] too, a good sort. He lets Sergeant Stanton worry about our day-to-day life, but he makes sure that the Navy petty officers could not assigns us to Navy-only duties.

One of the midshipmen, a Mr. Palmer, was particularly fond of trying to press Marines into doing Navy tasks. He was a right popinjay, barely 11 years old, giving orders like he was President Adams himself. I had to lies about my age to be able to enlist, but this child was not only allowed to serve, at $19 a month he makes almost twice as much as we Marines make.

Truth is that I wouldn't minds me some Navy jobs. Not the swabbing and splicing, mayhaps, but manning the capstan looks fun, and I would dearly loves to fire the six-pounders. Alls we normally do is stands sentry and drills, so something new would be most welcomed. But the lieutenant, he wants to makes sure we is not treated like extra sailor hands.

Even with that, I can't say life was bad. The *Enterprise* was a right plummy ship, and I was at ease with my place on it. Today, though, was my birthday, and I was 17 years old, still too young to be a Marine legal like. I didn't feels no different, though.

A call comes out from the tops. The lookout has spotted something. I looks, but I can't see nothing yet. But the captain, he can, what with his

---

[4] Swell: a gentleman

Jonathan P. Brazee

spyglass. He orders the ship to change course, and even before the ship comes around, Sergeant Stanton is on deck, yelling for me and those taking their morning shit to get below, get back into our dress uniforms, and get armed.

I changes uniforms and gets my Brown Bess, checking the flint to make sure it's all right and proper. When I gets back on deck, Mr. Lane's already there, and he tells us to go aloft. My post is on the tops of the fore topmast. It's not as steady as the main mast, but if the ships are closing, I gets the first shot in. Aside me's Hiram Whitaker, a New Jersey cobbler's son.

The *Enterprise* is not a big ship, just a schooner, only carrying 12 six-pound guns. With only two masts, me and Hiram's gots the fore topmast and Sterling Price and Hendrik Jacobsen the main mast. The rest of the Marines are on deck. If the Mahomatens gets on board, the others will be hand-to-hand. But if we gets hit, it's a long way to the hard deck.

I takes off my shoes. Lieutenant Lane frowns at that, him being a proper-type Marine, but I want my feet to grip the rigging. I'd rather be in me linen overalls to fight, but the captain wants us to look sharp to strikes fear into our foe. That's why Sergeant Stanton told us to change. All the captain has to do, though, is stand there presenting well. He's not climbing all over the rigging, what with the ship leaning this an' that ways.

I climbs up to the first yard, and here I does what's different. Our two tops are a mite small, and on the fore topmast, the sails can block the view. So I leaves the top to Hiram, and I lays down on the yard. I takes a line one of the tars gives me before, and I ties me onto the yard. Iffen I get hit, I won't be making the fall to the deck.

When I left the barracks, I thinks the drilling is over, but across the ocean to Gibraltar and for the last month blockading Tripoli, we drills and drills again. But now I'm grateful. I've practiced loading my Brown Bess lying on my belly. I loads the shot first, not the pan like in our drills, holding the musket below me, ramming it down from above 'stead of aside it like on land. Then I bring it up to prime the pan. A couple of the other Marines tried it my way, too, but only John Jericho could manage it. It takes a bit of strength, but it's no harder than what we do on dry land.

On the yard, I can shoots under the mainsail no matter how we are into the wind. And one more thing is that I figure the yard is a big spar, and iffen a shot comes my way, it will stop it 'fore it smashes into me.

22

I don't know iffen we're going to get into a tussle. We're supposed to be sailing to Malta for drinking water for the fleet. But I can see Lieutenant Sterett might be itching for a fight.

"Mr. Franklin, run up the British colors," I hears him say down on the deck below me.

The captain's a cunning shaver, God's truth. He also orders sailors who'll help us repel boarders to stand by just belowdecks, with only a small deck party and the Marines in sight.

It takes us round about half-an-hour to fall in on the other ship, a Tripolitan to be sure. She's bigger than us with 14 guns, but the captain, he don'care about that.

Lieutenant Sterett, with Mr. Franklin and our Lieutenant Crane asides him, calls out to the captain of the Tripolitan asking him whats he going to do.

The other captain calls back, "I'm looking for Americans, but I haven't found a one!"

"You have now!" our captain answered, then ordered a sailor to raise the American colors and for us to fire.

I was waiting for that, so I took a big fellow armed with a musket in my sights and fires. I feels a thrill when I sees him fall down, half of his neck gone. Our fusillade put three of the Mahomatens on the deck and the rest scrambles to action.

As we fire at them, they opens up a volley with seven of their six pounders, but not one hit us. Our captain had known what they'd do and has them at the wrong angle. Up in the tops, I wasn't in too much danger from their guns unless they de-mast us, but the poor tars in our gun holds, a direct shot could strikes them dead.

They missed us, but our tars are right on. We fires a broadside, holing her hull. She breaks away from us and tries to flee, but she's a slow girl, and she can't run off.

We forged ahead, tacking back into the wind and keeping the weather gauge. Most of the sailors were hard at work, turning the capstans to the orders of the captain while we danced with the other ship. I thinks we's more nimble, or maybe our captain be better, 'cause the next go-round, we comes up on her and fires a full broadside right up her fundamental, as Jacob calls it. I gets off another shot, but I don' know if I hits anyone.

She's taken some hits, and she knows she can't out-run us, so the Tripolitan luffs her sails and strikes her colors. We all gives three cheers 'cause victory is ours. I feels, well, I don' know how to says it. I feels like a real man now.

The captain brings us on a course to come alongside. I wants to see just how bad it's on that ship, but Sergeant Stanton yells out for us to stand alert. The Marines on the deck and about 10 sailors get ready to follow Lieutenant Crane onto the other ship when suddenly she hoists her colors again and fires muskets across our deck. With a yell, Mahomaten sailors rush to the side to throw grappling hooks.

With our Marines and sailors at the rails, they takes on the grapplers, but for me, I sees one popinjay officer shouting orders, sos I slowly aim in on him and squeeze my trigger. The officer goes down, and I feels another thrill. This is the second pirate I've kilt today, both fair shots as both ships sway an' pitch in the ocean. I may not have me long rifle, but the Brown Bess is doing fine for me.

Our six pounders open up again, but the Tripolitan's not done, an' the Arab sailors still try to bind us with grappling hooks. I can hears the guns below decks banging about as they get reloaded, so this time, it is up to us Marines. She tries to turn into us, and we all fire. I know I hits one of the sailors trying to grab us, and he falls like a sack of potatoes. All the Marines are firing, even Lt. Crane with his two pistols. I quickly reload and fires again, hitting the helmsman for sure. Another sailor jumps to the helm as she pulls away out of our fire. But that gives our six pounders another shot, and timber flies where the big balls smash.

I looks around as she pulls out of range. Not one Marine is hurt. Everyone has stood his ground.

Once again, it's the Navy's dance. We feint and turn for another 45 minutes before they make a mistake and we cross her, firing down her bow. I fires, too, but at 200 yards I probably didn't hit much of anything.

The Tripolitan strikes her colors again. This time, Lieutenant Sterett comes alongside from her stern, ready for treachery. Once again, just like last time, as we come to hail, she hoists her colors and tries to bind us to her. We all fires into her, driving the boarding sailors back. I sees maybe 15 or more lying dead on the deck, which is awash in blood. Several more are in poor shape, trying to get out of our fire.

Our six pounders offer a broadside, and an explosion on the other ship shows me our tars got one of their guns. A few of the sailors on the other ship fire muskets, and one round hits the spar I'm on, sending one small piece of wood into my cheek. I don't even brush back the bit of blood but continue my re-load before bringing my musket to bear one more time and firing. Through the smoke, I can't see if I've hit anything.

Again, we've pulled apart. The captain's back by the helm, calmly giving orders as if we was back on the Chesapeake coming up to Baltimore. His looks like a right painting of a Navy hero.

I don know what I thinks fighting would be, but I never thinks it will take this long. We've been fighting for maybe two hours, and we've closed four times, two of those when they says they want to surrender. I'm lying on this yard the whole time, and I needs to piss. But there's no time to climb down, and iffen I do it from here, I'm going to shower the Marines and tars below me.

I digs the splinter of wood out of my cheek. It's no bigger than a sewing needle. But I then feels for the hole in the spar. The ball hit it soundly, and a chunk of the spar's gone. Iffen that was my head, I'd have been making the acquaintance of Old Mr. Grim[5] for sure. I must have had the Angel Gabriel watching out for me. I looked back at Hiram, pointing at the hole. He just laughs.

It's a mite strange watching the Tripolitan just out of reach. I can sees the sailors, and I can sees the officers. But until we can bring our guns to bear or get close enough for the Marines to fire, they might as well be a hundred leagues away.

So far, no one on the *Enterprise* has been kilt. I thinks it must be God's work, with a little help from the captain, to be sure. Down below me, I can sees the determination in everyone's eyes. We sailed across the Atlantic Ocean to gets here, and now it's our turn to pays back the heathen pirates who dares to take our citizens and makes them slaves.

As we continue our dance, a lucky shot from one of our guns knocks off the Tripolitan's foremast yard, bringing down the mainsail. This will cripple her, and we's already the more nimble ship. She strikes her colors for a third time.

---

[5] Mr. Grim: death

It looks like she has to surrender, but the captain's ready for more treachery. He brings us up her port quarter, hailing the Tripolitan's captain. This time, the captain of the Tripolitan is at the rails, ready to hail back, so we relaxes just a bit. But yet again, it's a ruse, and she hoists her colors and fires at us, grappling hooks flying over the water. Two actually reach us, but quick thinking by a couple of sailors cut them free as we Marines pour fusillade after fusillade onto the other ship. I fires first at the captain, and I thinks I hit him, but he does not fall down dead.

Lieutenant Sterett's shouting to sink her, and a volley of six pounders hit her at the waterline. We continue to fire even as they throw down their arms and scream for mercy. One Mahomaten sailor takes their colors and throws them overboard and into the water. At that, the order comes for a cease-fire. We stop, but we don't relax.

Lieutenant Sterett calls out for the other captain to take a boat to us, but they tells us their boat is destroyed. The captain yells out for assurances that if we send someone over, they wont be murdered. Finally, he sends Lieutenant Crane, four Marines, ten sailors, and Mr. Palmer, the midshipman. Though only 11 years old and a right hobbadehay, I has to admits that the young lad was crazy brave during the fights, rushing to and fro along the rails, firing his pistols.

I stays up in the tops in case there is more treachery. But this time, the surrender is real. We kilt 30 of the Mahomatens and wounded another 30. The ship's surgeon and second lieutenant was dead, and the captain and first lieutenant was wounded. Our six pounders put 18 shots between the wind and the water, but most of the dead were from the musketry of us Marines.

I wants to board the ship, but I was ordered to stay aloft while our surgeon treats their wounded. The captain then has their masts cuts away and their guns thrown overboard. A spar is raised, and a tattered sail attached to it. It wouldn't do much, but it should get them ashore.

Not one American was kilt, and only one sailor is slightly wounded. Captain Sterett told us it was the most decisive victory in the history of the Navy.

As we broke away from the ship, we gives three loud huzzahs, proud of what we had done. The sailors, at best sometimes indifferent to us, even came to shakes our hands, saying without us the *Enterprise* surely would have been boarded.

As the sun began to set and we gets back underway for Malta, I realizes that my 17th birthday's one I will never forgets.

1802

When President Jefferson ordered the naval squadron, under Commodore Richard Dale, to sail to the Mediterranean, he had no authorization from Congress. It was not until he informed Congress of the battle between the *USS Enterprise* and the *Tripoli* that most of the legislative branch knew of the quasi state of war between the Barbary States and the US.

The first action of the war occurred when the *President* and the *Enterprise* sailed to Algiers, convincing the regent there to withdraw threats made against American shipping. The four-ship squadron then arrived off the coast of Tripoli, effecting a blockade of the port. A Greek ship was boarded by the crew of the *President* and a number of Tripolitan sailors were taken prisoner. These 43 prisoners were later exchanged for six American prisoners being held by the Pasha.

After the *Enterprise's* resounding victory, the *Tripoli* limped back into port. The Pasha was less than pleased. He had the ship's captain, Admiral Rais Mahomet Rous, paraded backwards on a donkey through the city streets while draped with sheep entrails, then given 500 bastinadoes (whippings) on the bottom of his feet.

The *Enterprise* was ordered back to Baltimore on October 3 with dispatches for the Secretary of the Navy. Upon arriving, Lieutenant Sterett was ordered to pay off and discharge the crew. The Marines on board went back to the barracks in Washington DC for further orders.

The severity of the Tripolitan defeat and of the admiral's punishment caused a drop of morale in the city, and recruitment of sailors suffered. In the United States, however, morale skyrocketed. Congress authorized a sword to be given to Lieutenant Sterett and a month's pay be given to each crew member. Several plays about the engagement were written and proved to be quite popular among the populace, even if the most popular one had the battle taking place in the English Channel with Lieutenant Sterett abandoning his English sweetheart for his duty to his country.

To begin the new year, on February 6, 1802, Congress finally authorized the action, essentially declaring war with "An act for the

Protection of Commerce and seamen of the United States against the Tripolitan cruisers, authorizing the President to "...employ such of the armed vessels of the United States as may be judged requisite... for protecting effectually the commerce and seamen thereof on the Atlantic ocean, the Mediterranean and adjoining seas." Whereas the *Enterprise* had to release the *Tripoli* after the battle, due to the fact that the US was not officially at war, the act now allowed for all Tripolitan vessels to be taken as prizes.

In April of 1802, Commodore Dale's squadron returned to the US. Commodore Richard Morris was chosen to lead the second squadron to the Mediterranean.

On June 17, 1802, the Emperor of Morocco declared war on the United States, but he accepted a peace treaty in August.

1802 was the beginning of what President Jefferson called "The Two Years Sleep" with regard to the war.

Chapter 5

Baltimore Navy Yard
April 1802

Jacob

I came down the gangway with a spring in my step. All my worldly possessions were wrapped up in my blanket, but I was free, and that's what counted. I peered ahead onto the dock, and not only was Ichabod there waiting, but Seth as well.

The *United States* and the *Philadelphia* had made the crossing together, so I expected Ichabod, but Seth's ship had returned home about eight months ago. I was sure happy to see him, though. I jumped off the end of the gangway, landing with both feet together on the dock. It was good to get off the ship.

Both of my friends stood there waiting for me, and I tried to be nonchalant, but I ended up running the last 10 yards to give both of them hugs, pounding on their backs.

"What are you doing here?" I asked Seth. "I figured you'd be back in Pennsylvania, feet in the dirt."

Seth's eyes clouded a bit before he responded. "You knows there's nothing for me there. I'm staying right here in the Marines. I came up from the barracks with one of the wagons they hires to haul all of you back there."

"Not me, though," I told him. "I'm done, and I'm going home. I mustered out already with our lieutenant."

With Congress pressuring President Jefferson on the budget and the cost of the war, he had directed the commandant to reduce the size of the Corps. I enlisted for three years like the rest, but as he had to slash the Corps almost in half, he had authorized early dismissals upon request. I had decided to take the Corps up on that opportunity.

"So you decided that for sure, I guess," Ichabod said. "I know you told me you might back in Gibraltar, but I'm surprised you did it."

"Why not?" I asked. "I've got almost a hundred dollars here," I said pointing at my belly where I had wrapped my wages for the last year. "I'm a regular swell now."

Both laughed. One hundred dollars does not make a man rich, but for me, that's a lot of money. It was enough to do what I want, at the very least.

I'm not surprised that Seth decided to stay on. I'd heard he had done well on the *Enterprise*, and all the crew had been slated an extra month's pay for their defeat of the *Tripoli*. I think he was born for the military life.

I looked to Ichabod, eyebrows raised in a silent question.

"I'm staying, too," he told me. "I'm no hero like our young lad here, but I like the life. I'm not asking for a discharge."

I had been happy to see the two of them, but suddenly I realized that this meant we would probably not see each other again. That sobered me up. These were my friends, my brothers. I had made new friends aboard the *United States*, of course, but none of them shared the same bond with me as these two men.

"You saves a hundert dollar? I has maybe $5 left to me," Seth said ruefully.

"Well you spent most of yours in the nanny houses of Malta and Gibraltar, near as I've heard. Even the tars were impressed," I told him.

His face reddened and Ichabod laughed, punching the young man in the arm.

"Well, what else is I going to do with the kelter?" he mumbled. "I gots it, so I spends it."

"A hundred dollars is pretty impressive, though," Ichabod said.

"I never bought tobacco, and I had only a mite of ale when we went ashore. I had to buy a new hat when mine went overboard, and I had to pay $4 for a new jacket."

The hats looked good when they were new, but they quickly cracked and split, and keeping one on became a Herculean task. Most of us lost them overboard. The new ones were made in France, and they stood up to the sea life better, but that put me $1.45 back.

Ichabod reached over to finger my blue jacket.

"That's right good quality," he observed.

"The commodore wanted us in our uniforms all the time, and after a month, we were looking pretty scurrilous. So the lieutenant wrote back to the commandant, and he was told to buy some Russian duck, then have new jackets made. We had to buy them, though. The lieutenant said he would try to petition the commandant for redress, but I don't give that much hope."

"You going to keep it?" Ichabod asked.

"I'll happily sell it for $2, if you know anyone who can wear it. I would've been happy with overalls or even sailor clothes, but the commodore liked his Marines to look sharp, hair powdered, our muskets gleaming. On shore, we escorted him to show off to the British, but even at sea on sentry duty outside his stateroom, we couldn't have a hair out of place. The sergeants had to inspect each of us before we went on post."

"Hair powdered?" Ichabod asked. "Did you have powder?"

"Yes. Lieutenant Keene had the commodore's ear, and he was able to get a full tin that he gave to Lieutenant Fenwick. Sergeant Smith kept it, and he issued out powder like a sergeant quartermaster. I'm surprised he didn't make us sign a chit for it each time."

"To you good fortune, then. On the *Philadelphia*, we had to use flour that we got at Leghorn. I don't mind being a bounce[6], especially when there's ewes prancing about, but I want proper powder, not flour that clumps when I sweat. I'm a Marine, not a baker."

"No powder for us," Seth added. "Lieutenant Sterett made us looks the bounce, too, when we's on sentry, but he says powder can only foul a fellow's eyes in battle."

That surprised me. I have respect of most of the Naval officers I met, but with their honor and so forth and their stupid dueling, they often put appearances over that of practicality.

A sergeant came up, asking Seth if his wagon was loaded. He called him "Seth," not Private Crocker, and that familiarity struck me wrong. I was surprised that I felt a small pang of jealousy. Sergeants were sergeants, above us. Privates needed to band together. Even if I was leaving, I wanted Seth to be my friend, not the friend of some unknown sergeant.

---

[6] Bounce: a man who dresses smartly

"I guess I gots to get moving. We wants to get back afore midnight, so we needs to head out."

While we were talking, most of the Marines from the frigates had clamored aboard one of the six wagons. The officers had already boarded carriages and had moved off, but the weather was good, so the wagons would be fine for the privates and NCO's.

I felt a bit of wetness welling up in my eyes, so I reached out and firmly grasped first Ichabod, then Seth in a forearm shake. Men shake like that. They don't cry.

They loaded the wagons, joining those already on board. Both waved to me as the line of wagons moved out, ready for the long trip down to Washington. I waited until they were out of sight before shouldering my blanket-pack and leaving the Navy Yard.

Jonathan P. Brazee

Chapter 6

USS Chesapeake
In Port at Naples, Italy

December 18, 1802

Ichabod

"But I want to fight someone! I didn't join the Marines to sit on my cheeks," Achilles shouted, feeling the effects of too much wine.

Achilles was a small lad, thinner than a rake. Being the "old salt" that I am, what with one whole deployment in back of me, I had latched onto the boy as we first came on board the ship, took him under my wings, and most importantly, had him string his hammock next to mine. When I was sleeping, I didn't want a gundiguts[7] next to me, bumping me with each movement of the ship. With Achilles, while we still might bump our bumfiddles through the hammocks, it was not like we were lying together like man and wife.

After maneuvering him to bunk next to me, he latched onto me like a gosling to the goose, and as we had orders to go ashore in groups no smaller than four, Achilles was as good as anyone else. Together with Sam Truxton and Jericho Alden, the four of us had just spent an enjoyable evening at our favorite nanny house, enjoying the company of the women of the town. I had sentry duty coming up, so I drank no wine, but the other three had no such restrictions.

"Easy, my lad. If we were off the Tripolitan shores, we'd have no such time as this, with fair-roe-buck[8] short-heeled women[9] and wine.

---

[7] Gundigut: a fat person
[8] Fair-roe-buck: beautiful
[9] Short-helled-woman: a prostitute

We'd only see each other for company, and I must tell you, I find you not the least attractive!" I told him.

The other two laughed, but young Achilles was on a roll.

"I speak the truth," he protested. "I want to close with the Mahomaten and show him what a Charleston man can do!"

I was quite happy to be spending my time in Leghorn, in Malta, in Malaga, in Naples, and most of all, in Livonine. We passed into the Mediterranean on May 25, but as of yet, we had not made any appearance off the Barbary Coast. A small part of me wondered what actual combat would be like, but the rest of me was quite happy at the easy life we led. Not one member of the squadron had died as a result of the enemy. We had a few die of natural causes, and several officers, including Captain McKnight, a Marine on the *Constellation*, were killed in duels with each other or the British, but to date this was a most pleasant cruise.

A group of three British sailors passed by, one making what had to be a crude comment, even if I could not hear the words. But we ignored them, under strict orders not to get into a rumble. We weren't officers, so we didn't have their crazy ideas of the defense of honor. You didn't see privates or seamen dueling it out until one was dead.

Achilles was somewhat of a rumbuptious lad, so alone, he might have gotten into a fight, especially as cup-shot[10] as he was, but with us there, we were able to keep things calm. Achilles might weigh 120 pounds, but he had more fire in him than any wildcat.

We came up to the ship and prepared to board. David England was the gangway sentry, and along with one of the ship's petty officers, they managed who came on board and who went ashore. As we were signing in, a low rumble sounded, followed by a vile stink.

"Bother round mouth speaks!" shouted Sam as he shoved Jericho while the rest of us expressed our displeasure.

Jericho laughed at his virulence and stepped up to report his return. Private England and the petty officer had to ignore the stench as the sailor logged Jericho's return, although the petty officer looked daggers at him.

Crude and coarse language and humor were part of life in the military, perhaps even more so aboard a ship where we were in each others' laps most of the time. It was true in my first war, and it remained

---

[10] Cub-shot: drunk

true in this one. I would never josh about bodily functions in proper society, one with women about, but here, it seemed natural. Only two nights ago, there had been an impromptu farting contest in berthing, with one Marine after another letting out volcanic blasts. I forsook to join myself, but I laughed as heartily as the rest until we crowned Jericho as the winner.

I made my way down to berthing and began to wash. Even at port, we were allotted only 5 quarts of water a day, so I had to be judicious. I might have skipped using the water, but Commodore Morris was even more pernicious as to the appearance of "his" Marines when they were on duty than most any other officer. At least on the *Chesapeake*, we had actual hair powder, not flour. I applied it, checking myself in the small mirror before carefully pulling on my jacket.

I knew the sergeant of the watch would check me before I went on duty, but I wanted to look as bounce as possible before then. I asked Achilles to look me over, but as cup-shot as he was, he didn't do me much good. I left him collapsed in his hammock, still clothed and shod.

Before going on deck, I went to the armory and drew my musket. At sea, we often kept our muskets close at hand, but in port, the commodore wanted the weapons out of easy reach. I went back topside and waited for inspection. I wondered how many inspections I had done over the years, both in the Army and in the Marines. It could be my age or my memory, but I think that the Marines took inspections much more seriously than the Continental Army.

The rest of the watch section milled about until the sergeant of the watch came up and called us to order. He inspected us, but as it was evening, not surprisingly, no officer was there as well. We had too many captains and lieutenants on board, and without much to do, they tended to get into our NCOs' business. But they were all probably ashore now, enjoying whatever officers enjoy when they are off duty.

We passed the muster and were marched to our posts. I had the commodore's cabin. He sometimes stayed ashore, but ashore or on board, he wanted a Marine outside his door at all times. I relieved William Perkins just as the ship's bells sounded. I now had four hours of boredom to get through.

A veteran of countless watches, I had the ability to leave my body standing, but to send my mind out into the world. I had spent many hours contemplating my past. Unfortunately, not much was there about which to be proud. Yes, I served with General Washington, but that was the highlight of my life. I worked as a farm-hand, something I never told Seth; I worked mucking out stables. I worked as a tanner. I tried my hand at business, failing twice. I fell in love once, but she was more in love with what little I had saved, and when that was gone, so was she. In short, I have left no mark on the world. When Mr. Grim comes to visit me and I'm shoveled, no one will miss me, no one will shed any tears.

I'm pushing 50 years of age, and it is rough when a man realizes his life has been for naught. It's a dagger to the heart. I still want to make my mark on the world, but for now, it's easier to just mark time as a Marine, to be part of this young organization, even if it seems to be the bastard child of the sea service.

I was brought out of my reverie as the commodore and his wife approached. I came to attention and presented arms, face devoid of emotion.

The commodore simply nodded at me, but the "commodoress," as we called her, smiled and said "Thank you, Private Cone."

The commodoress was not the only woman on board the ship. There were several other wives on board, and the commodore's maid, Sal, helped care for his baby son Gerald. Furthermore, the commodoress was most probably up the duff,[11] and that happened after we set sail.

She was a lady, though, through and through, and she seemed to know the name of each member of the crew. I couldn't say she was a handsome woman. Mr. Wadsworth, one of the midshipmen, described her along the lines of being not beautiful, but looking "very well in a veil." But it still didn't seem right that she was here on a warship. Granted, we have yet to see any fighting, but we certainly would have to at some point.

A sentry is blind and deaf except to danger. What goes on in the commodore's cabin is not for a mere private's eyes and ears. The high and mighties don't consider us as people, so they say things, do things, as if we weren't there. We learn to ignore, to keep things close to the vest.

Tonight, it was only the commodore and his wife in the cabin, no meetings with the other officers. Evidently, at dinner, the commodore was asked when he would be taking the squadron to Tripoli. He replied that it

---

[11] Up the duff: pregnant

was getting late in the season and that the Tripolitan ships would be stuck in the harbor until spring, so he would be staying here in Italy. Once in his cabin, he asked his wife what she thought of his answer. Her voice was quieter, so I could not hear her response, but to me, it seemed as if the commodore wanted confirmation of his decision.

Eventually, the talking died down, soon to be replaced by the sounds of screwing. This was usually the case. The commodoress might be hatchet-faced, but she loved her shagging, and the commodore was evidently her stallion. Being in the pudding[12] club[13] didn't seem to matter none to her, and probably wouldn't until the little one popped out a few months from now, a true "son of a gun," as the saying goes.

I had just visited the nanny house myself, so I was not bothered, but on the long passage across the ocean, such duties could make a man's mind wander. I let my mind go blank again and left the commodore and commodoress to their congress.

---

[12] Pudding: stomach
[13] Pudding club: pregnant

1803

For most of 1802 and the first half of 1803, little was done in pursuit of the war. Commodore Richard Morris led his Second Mediterranean Squadron not to the Barbary Shores, as was his orders, but to ports in England, Gibraltar, Italy, and Malta. When asked when he would sail to Tripoli, he had excuses but no action.

On July 22, the *USS Constellation*, under the command of Captain Alexander Murray, engaged a Tripolitan galley and eight gunboats, sinking two of them.

William Eaton, the counsel to Tunis, advocated taking a tougher stand against the Barbary States. Frustrated with Commodore Morris' lack of action, he declared on August 1, 1802 to Hamet Qaramanli that Tripoli was under blockade. Merchant masters, afraid of conflict, simply refused cargo consignments for Tripoli. Without a ship within 300 leagues of Tripoli, he effected a virtual blockade as almost all provisions and trade for Tripoli came via Tunis.

The *USS Enterprise* seized the Tunisian imperial ship *Paulina* on January 15, 1803, when it attempted to run the blockade into Tripoli. The *Paulina's* captain insisted that he was only dropping off passengers. The Tunisian bey, Hamouda Pacha, threatened war if the ship was not returned and damages paid.

On February 22, 1803, under the summons of William Eaton, the first ships of the squadron made an appearance at a Barbary port when the *Chesapeake*, *New York*, and *John Adams* sailed into Tunis Harbor. Commodore Morris initially demanded that the *Paulina* go to prize court, but he quickly capitulated to all of the Tunisian demands, paying for items not even on the initial grievance. When attempting to return to his ship, Commodore Morris, Captain Rodgers, Mr. Eaton, and Mr. Cathcart, a former slave and now assistant to Eaton, were arrested and brought back to the palace where the bey demanded $34,000 that he said was a loan to Eaton. Eaton had borrowed the money to send to the Hamet Karmanli, the deposed Tripolitan ruler, but denied obligating the Navy to pay it back.

Jonathan P. Brazee

Commodore Morris acquiesced and paid the amount, and the five men were released.

Commodore Morris transferred his command to the *USS New York* on March 23.

On May 13, the *USS John Adams* captured the Tripolitan 20-gun ship *Meshuda* without resistance as she attempted to slip into port under a Moroccan flag.

On May 23, Lieutenant David Porter led a party of 50 Marines and sailors from the *USS New York* and *Enterprise* in an attempt to burn some feluccas beached near Tripoli. They managed to fire the grain boats, but abandoned them too soon, and the Tripolitans were able to extinguish the fires. There were 15 American casualties.

On June 7, Commodore Morris finally arrived in Tripoli. Under a white flag, he met with the Pasha, who demanded $250,000 plus $20,000 per year to pay for the cost of the war. Morris, unsure of what to do and without authority to negotiate, sailed for Gibraltar.

Frustrated with Morris' lack of action, President Jefferson ordered him relieved of command on June 21. Commodore Morris did not learn of this until August 31 when he was met by Captain Hugh Campbell of the *USS John Adams* at Malaga, Spain and handed a letter from the Navy Secretary telling him that he "could consider himself suspended in the command of the squadron…and of the Frigate, the *New York*."

The *USS John Adams* and the *USS Enterprise* engaged a Tripolitan polacre of 22 guns, the Tripolitan's largest ship, several miles west of Tripoli on June 22. After a short action, the Tripolitans abandoned their ship, which was destroyed in a huge explosion before the Americans could board her.

Fearful of a war with Morocco and not yet knowing he had been relieved of command, and believing that the Tripolitan threat had been extinguished, Commodore Morris lifted the blockade of Tripoli on June 26.

Two days after entering the Mediterranean on August 26, the *USS Philadelphia* captured the Moroccan ship *Mirboha* and the American prize *Celia*, which it had under tow.

Commodore Preble arrived in the Mediterranean on September 13.

Chapter 7

USS Enterprise
June 1, 1803

Seth

I looks ahead hoping that the Mahomatens were still there. We were running back after we signals the *New York* that we found ten Tripolitan boats unloading grain on shore, and we left the *John Adams* there to loft a few shots at them to keep them occupied. There was about 1,000 men on shore, with foot and cavalry, and a stone fort. Us being the fastest ship, we has to go fetch the *New York*. Now, we may be getting in a good rumble.

This year's been nothing like our fight with the *Tripoli*. The ship has been good luck, and I likes Lieutenant Lane and even Lieutenant Sterett, who can be a hard man, so I comes back this time to my Navy home. Some of the tars were the same as was onboard before, and we work better together.

In January, we takes the ship *Paulina*. I was hoping for another prize payment, but that causes all sorts of problems, and the commodore hisself has to go to Tunis to fix things up.

After that, we gets a new captain, Lieutenant Issac Hull. The new captain's a bit of a gundiguts, but he's a fighter for all that. He also says that sailors and Marines do not need to be flogged for every little thing. He and Lieutenant Lawrence, the ship's first lieutenant, they gots the crew happy and working hard.

The first action we see with the new captain is a week ago when we trap a Tripolitan on the shore. I thoughts that we was going to raid it, and we Marines gots ready, but the captain tells Lieutenant Lane that we have to wait for permission, and then the commodore, he says we can't risk life for a small target. We've been aboard ship for several weeks, so we wants to fight, but no one listens to us Marines much no how.

Jonathan P. Brazee

A couple of days later, we sees nine gunboats near the new battery the Tripolitans has built. We gets the *New York* and the *John Adams*, and the commodore decides we gots to sail in together. Only thing is we never practices that. The wind dies, and we sit there in each other's way. The *John Adams* tries to get some broadsides off, but the *New York*, when she wants to fire, she fires right through the *John Adams*, one shot cutting her foretop-gallant bowline.

Our master-at-arms, an old bald tar by the name of Wiggins, says that if the Tripolitans row out to us, they can take us, so we Marines better be ready. But the Mahomatens just stay ashore until a breeze comes up and we pull away.

Yesterday, we fires on another ship, but nothing happens. All of us, tars and Marines, are ready for a pummel. No more larking around.

We arrives afore the *New York*, of course, and then watches the shore. The boats is still unloading, and they has cavalry and foot there. I wants to do something, but Lieutenant Lane says we needs to wait for orders.

Finally, at about 5:00 PM, all three ships are ready, but the commodore, he decides to be a gentleman and gives them until midnight to comes alongside his ship or he'll burn them. Lieutenant Porter on the *New York*, he wants to attack, but the commodore won't do it. But he does lets a reconnaissance mission go. Mr. Porter, Midshipman Wadsworth, another tar, four Marines get in one jolly boat and Lieutenant Lane takes four of us on another jolly boat to go have a look see. Of course, I is one of the Marines in our jolly boat.

All of us have our musket, a cutlass, and two pistols. I can shoots the pistol fine, but I might needs more practice with the cutlass. That's a weapon for officers and NCOs, not for privates like me.

We gets all quiet and rows up behind their boats. We can hears them speaking their language, but then someone spies us and they fire. We fire back and pull hard away. We gets to a small island only a quarter mile off, and get out. We is standing on Tripoli.

Mr. Wadsworth, he's a frisky lad, and he has us laughing. He stands on the highest rock, pointing his hand in the air, then brings it down like he's planting a flag. He declares the rock for the United States and President Jefferson.

42

We waits until midnight like the commodore wants, then rows back. We gets back on the *Enterprise* and waits there, too. Then a message comes over. We're going to attack at dawn.

I checks my weapons and powder, then climb into my hammock for a mite of doss.[14]

"Shouldn't we get ready?" Justice Frey asks me, shaking my hammock.

Justice is young, only 18, and he looks to everyone else for answers. This'll be his first fight, and I can tells he's nervous.

"I'm ready, and now I wants to be rested whens we rumble, so lets me sleep."

I can tells he wants to ask more, but the devil's look I gives him makes him go find someone else to bother.

Sergeant Cooper comes in later and wakes us up. We get dressed, making sure we look bounce. Then we checks our muskets again. I keeps the pistols with me, and the cutlass. Who knows if I needs them today?

I goes on deck, and the captain is giving Mr. Lane and Mr. Lawrence orders. We're going to be under the command of Lieutenant Porter again, but Lieutenant Hull, he wants to make sure the *Enterprise* is served well.

We've got two jolly boats this time, and we climb down inside. Aside of all the Marines, we gots the yeoman of the powder room, the ship's armorer, two quarter gunners, and the Master-at-Arms. We also gots barrels of black powder. In my boat is only Marines, but the other boat has the tars and a couple of Marines to helps them. When the *New York* sounds eight bells, we shove off and begin the row to the shore.

As we comes up, the Mahomatens blunder and shout, but our musket fire keeps them away from the four fire boats. Some of the cavalry, though, they scream and shout, then comes in close and fire. One Mahomaten, on a black stallion, comes a mite too close. I aims at him and fires. He falls off the back of his horse in a cloud of sand and lays still. One of the tars in another boat claims the kill, but I hears him fire after the Mahomaten was already falling kilt. This Tripolitan is mine.

Shot from the ship goes over our heads and hits the shore, killing foot and cavalry, but they do not backs down. Our own shot is running low, and Mr. Porter stands up in the boat next to us, shouting for the

---

[14] Doss: sleep

fireboats to hurry. Then I sees him stagger, shot in the left thigh. Rights again, another shot hits his right thigh, and he goes down.

At last flames begin to lick at the boats. We's out of shot, so Mr. Lawrence, he's taking command, and he orders us to pull for the ships. As soon as we's out of musket range, the Tripolitans rush back to their boats to fight the fires. The ships give them good cannonade, but they manages to puts out the fires before the boats is sunk. I hears our yeoman of the powder says that the grain keeps the fires from burning fast.

As I climbs back onto our ship, I looks back. Some of the boats are burnt, some not. Three still have masts up. We pummels them but good, but not kilt them.

We went to attack with 50 men in nine jolly boats. Fifteen men were hurt by the Mahomatens, but none kilt, and all boats returns safely. I wishes we sinks all ten boats, though.

Chapter 8

Princeton, NJ
Aug 5, 1803

Jacob

"My friend Seth was probably there!" I told Suva, reading the account of the attack on the Tripolitan boats. "He's on the *Enterprise*!"

Although it had been a year, I still eagerly followed any news of the war with Tripoli. There hadn't been much reported lately, but the article in *The Independent Gazetteer* gave a stirring account of the battle. No mention was made of any Marines, but Lieutenant David Porter was now a national hero.

Suva looked at me from her small chair where she was doing her sewing. I wished she didn't have to take in work like that, but I was doing poorly in finding employment. If it wasn't for the largess of her aunt, we would have been on the street by now. But a gable in the house of a man's wife's aunt is hardly a real home. I felt like I had let Suva down.

When I had come back from sea with a hundred dollars in my pocket and asked her to marry me, it seemed as if our future was clear. But that money was long gone, and we were both lowered to scraping for pennies. The newspaper I had was from three days ago, something I picked up abandoned on the street.

"Husband," she said, something that still gave me a thrill each time the words crossed her lips, "I think that maybe it is time to reconsider mustering up again."

"No!" I almost shouted, ashamed as that made her flinch back. "We've talked about this. I cannot leave you alone."

"You are my dearest one, but I know you want to go. Please, look me in the eyes and tell me that is not true."

I could not do that. For the last six months, I had often thought of going back into the Marines. I had missed several recruitment drives, and

Jonathan P. Brazee

most of Commodore Preble's squadron had already sailed. But I couldn't leave my young wife alone to fend for herself.

"I thought as much." She came over to take my hands in hers. "I do not want you gone from me, or in harm's way. But I am safe here with my aunt. I know you want to go, and with ten dollars a month, we can save again. Once this war's over, then trade will pick up again, and jobs will be plentiful once more. With God's grace, I am sure of it."

I wasn't sure what to say. I did not want to leave her, but my thoughts often drifted across the ocean where my brothers were fighting.

"Didn't you say there's still a ship here that's not yet left?"

"No, that was the *Philadelphia*. It pulled out last week. My friend Ichabod is on her. But there is one more, the *Argus*, up in Boston."

I didn't tell her that I had the recruiting bill in my pocket, one I had taken off the board at the Navy Yard last week when I was looking for work in Philadelphia. I took it after I had watched a Marine fifer and two drummers march in a recruitment parade, and I had felt something digging at my very soul as I watched them. After that, I had talked to the recruiting sergeant there, and he had assured me of a posting on the *Argus* if I but signed the enlistment papers.

"So go. Do what you must, and I will be fine back here. We will be reunited again soon, and then we can start our life anew."

I pulled her in close, my face buried in her belly. I loved this woman, and I wanted to be with her, but I also wanted to be at sea, back with the Marines. If I had a good job, I wouldn't consider it, but a starving man has few options.

It was strange that I was so happy to muster out in Baltimore nigh 15 months ago, but now, I missed the life.

I looked up and into my wife's eyes. I could see no subterfuge there. She was earnest and willing. That was enough. I think I had made up my mind some time ago, only now I could admit it to myself. I was going to be a Marine again.

Chapter 9

USS Philadelphia
August 21, 1803

Ichabod

"John House just died," Corporal Simms told us as he entered our berthing spaces.

We took that in silence for a moment. I hadn't known John that well yet, but he was a young, robust man, and to think that in two days he was gone was a bit much to absorb.

"They treat us as chattel, worse than an officer's dog," William Ray said as others nodded in agreement. "The surgeon's mate wouldn't deign to treat a sick Marine."

William had a dim view on life aboard the *Philadelphia*. A former teacher and businessman who had gone bankrupt, he had to leave his wife and sign on with the Marines when he couldn't get other work. At 34, he was older than most of the other privates, and so he gravitated to me. I tried to call him Will, but he insisted on William.

Despite his debts, I was surprised he had enlisted. He was a bit of a Tom Thumb, standing about 5'4", and he couldn't have weighed over 135 pounds. He was not skilled with our Charlevilles, and climbing the tops got him all afeerd. More than once, he told me he was smarter than all the officers together. For all of that, he was bene cove[15], and I liked his company.

His point was valid, though. The *Philadelphia* was a 36-gun Class 1 Frigate, with over 200 enlisted sailors on board. We had 41 Marines and over 30 NCO's and officers. Other than Lieutenant Osborne, I didn't even know what the other lieutenants and captains did.

---

[15] Bene cove: a good guy

Jonathan P. Brazee

With so many Marines, the sailors felt we didn't do enough to run the ship, and they resented the fact that our officers kept us to Marine duties. So feelings were a mite tense between the Navy and Marines. Captain Bainbridge was a bit of a tyrant, given to rages, and he too easily took the word of his subordinates, but Mr. Cox, the first lieutenant, had kind words for the Marines. For the most part, though, the bluejackets and Marines stayed apart.

William took out his notebook and wrote something down. He fancied hisself a writer, so he was always jotting down things. He looked at what he had written before, and like he was reminded, he complained again.

"How can a midshipman order punishment to a man old enough to be his grandfather, one who bled in the war?" he asked to no one in particular.

He was referring to Peter Whelan, a man 28 years in the Army, who was wounded seven times in the revolution and another three times in St. Claire's defeat, a man who came highly recommended by General Wilkinson hisself.

Peter had nodded off on post. The Marines were split into two watches, but even if off-duty, we were kept awake during the day. Most times, we had but four hours of sleep each day, and with hard toil, it was difficult to keep awake. The snotty caught Peter, then had him dragged off in chains. Three days later, he was brought back on deck to receive his flogging with Thomas Higgins, a sailor who had a bucket of water thrown on him in his hammock by another snotty. When Thomas told the midshipman that he didn't think a gentleman would do such a deed, the little tyrant flew into a rage and reported to the officer of the deck that he had been insulted.

Some midshipmen, such as Mr. Gamble, were proper young gentlemen, but others were unbearable. When a Marine answers to muster, he is taught to respond with "Here" rather than the "Here, sir" that a sailor uses. One night, a midshipman was sent to our berthing for yet one more muster. Most of us remembered to add the "sir" to our response, but two Marines, mayhaps befuddled with sleep, merely responded with "Here." The little unlicked cub flew into such a rage that he took hisself a mizzen line and proceeded to beat the two Marines 20 or 30 times each as hard as his spindly arms could strike. Luckily he was no Hercules or the Marines would have been killed. Our sergeant reported this to the Lieutenant of Marines, but there was no satisfaction returned.

Punishment seemed to be the foremost complaint with William, and rightly so. David Burling was still in irons for sleeping on post, and Captain Bainbridge had been heard to say he would take "infinite pleasure to see him hanging from the yard arm." We didn't know if that was legal unless the ship was in a place of danger, not just crossing the Atlantic Ocean, and Sergeant McElroy told us Mr. Osborn was pleading David's case. I surely did not want to hear the drums beat punishment call and watch a dangle[16] done, 'specially on a Marine I know and like.

Despite the punishment, despite the lack of sleep, life on the *Philadelphia* was good. We had plenty of food. Sundays, Tuesdays, and Thursdays, we got one and a half pounds of beef, and Mondays, Wednesdays, and Saturdays, we got a pound of pork. That's more meat than I've had in many years. We got our daily ration of rum, even if the purser's steward tried to keep it for himself too oft.

"I aver that if the farmers knew their tax dollars were being spent to flog sailors and Marines, they would have something to say about that," William went on.

Truth is I didn't even know what "aver" means, still don't, but I guessed it just meant "say." As I mentioned before, William was a former teacher who thought he was a writer, and he tended to use words not many of us would know. At least I had some schooling. Some of the lads here barely spoke good English.

"William," I told him, "you're a private of Marines, not President Jefferson. You're going to give yourself a fit unless you learn to just bend over and take it in the feak like a good boy."

He turned to look at me in astonishment.

"You tell me that you accept when the purser charges us 50 cents for a pound of tobacco when the very regulations they use to justify beating us affirms that he should charge us ten cents a pound? You accept that an officer on board this very ship beats a sailor to death in Baltimore, and nothing is done?"

"No, but I don't accept Mahomaten pirates making slaves out of good Americans, either, or that the British can impress American sailors,

---

[16] Dangle: a hanging

or that yellow fever can lay low a city. But sometimes, we have to accept the facts of life. A deer can complain about the wolf, but it won't change nature. You saw what happened to Sergeant Timmons when he tried to complain about the purser's steward keeping our rum. He received nigh on 30 lashes. This was a sergeant, not a private like me and you."

Several of the other Marines turned to William to hear his response. Most of the others, mayhaps all of them, understood their position in life better than poor William. We were privates, lower than seamen. If we accepted that, then we could be at peace with ourselves.

"If we don't say anything, then nothing will change. We profess to hate the British, yet we copy all things British. Our Navy is just a poor reflection of the Royal Navy when we have the chance to make it into something far better. We shouldn't copy them, warts and all."

I didn't have time to respond back, not that I think William would accept my opinions. The drum beat general quarters, and we all rushed above decks, ready for battle. And battle we did. For the next two hours, under the orders of Mr. Cox, we rushed to and fro over the deck, fighting imaginary foes. We Marines had our muskets and bayonets, but the sailors had pistols, belaying pins, axes, pikes, and anything else they could grab. It was a wonder that no one was hurt in all the rigmarole, but I "averred" that if we could fight the Tripolitan with as much fierceness as we displayed to the wind and waves, then we would own the bashaw's palace by Christmas!

Chapter 10

USS Philadelphia
Gibraltar
August 28, 1803

Ichabod

"That was sumptin, there, Ichabod." Achilles pounded on my back as he returned from the *Mirboha,* where he had been while the prize was brought back to Gibraltar.

Two days ago, at last, I had been part of the taking of an enemy ship. We had just arrived in Gibraltar on the 24th, but as soon as the captain heard of a Moroccan ship just offshore, we headed back out to sea to find her, and find her we did. She was the *Mirboha,* a 22-gun frigate, and she had her own prize, the American ship *Celia* in trace. At first, the Moroccan commander tried to tell us the *Celia* was just sailing with her, but the captain smelled rotten fish in that. Over the Moroccan's protest, he sent a party over, to include us Marines, and we found Mr. Owen, the *Celia's* captain, and some crewmen below decks in chains. I thought the fight would be fiercer, but after much caterwauling, the Moroccan crew just gave up and let us take her. We transferred some of the prisoners to the *Philadelphia,* and Mr. Cox and Mr. Macdonough took some sailors and eight Marines on the *Mirboha* as the prize crew.

As I stood guard over them, one sailor kept looking up at me with sad eyes, drawing his finger across his throat. I 'spect he thought we were going to kill the entire crew.

Achilles was happier than a pig in a corn crib. He had followed me to the *Philadelphia,* and at last he felt like we had done something worthwhile.

"Those Mahomatens, they were happy to know we wasn't going to just out and kill them, and after that, all they wanted was food and rum. I thought you said Mahomatens don't eat no pork or drink hard spirits, but they sure did a good job putting both down on the way back here."

Jacob had told me and Seth some on the Muslim religion, and I know he said they don' eat pork, like the Jew, but unlike them and us, they don' drink spirits either. I was going to talk to him about that if we ever met again. It seems like they were just like everyone else, after all.

"I heard Mr. Cox's going to stay on that ship as prize captain, and Mr. Porter from the *New York* is going to take his place here," he went on, voice now lower.

We'd heard it, too, already. All the Marines liked Mr. Cox, and Mr. Porter had a reputation that was none too flattering, so none of us was all too happy about it. We already heard about his being shot at Tripoli, and you couldn't deny he was a doughty fighter, but he treated sailors and Marines poorly, and there were other black rumors I didn't want to give credence to. Mr. Macdonough, too, was a good officer, one of the older midshipmen, just waiting for to become a lieutenant. Losing both Cox and Macdonough would make things tougher on board the *Philadelphia*.

It weren't up to us, though, so like good Marines, we would just do our duty no matter the ship's officers. Mr. Osborne asked for volunteers to stay with the *Mirboha* while they waited for prize court, and I thought about it for a bit before deciding that I like big ships under my feet, and the *Philadelphia* was that. When I decided to stay, Achilles decided to stay as well.

Anyhoo, I came on this voyage to fight, not sit in Gibraltar for months. I thought that the *Philadelphia* offered more chances at adventure.

Chapter 11

USS Philadelphia
Off Tripoli Harbor
October 31, 1803

Ichabod

The drum called for reporting to battle stations at about 9:00 in the morning. The lookout had spotted a xebec trying to run our blockade, so we were going in to the attack. The captain wanted to take her as a prize. We fired off a few rounds from our 18-pounders, but the smaller ship hugged the coastline while trying to reach the harbor.

The *Philadelphia* and the *Vixen* had been on blockade duty for three weeks while Commodore Preble sailed to force Emperor Souleiman of Morocco to sue for peace. Captain Bainbridge's plan was to use the *Vixen* to flush out the Tripolitans hugging the shore; then our big *Philadelphia* could force the action. Today, though, we were alone, as the *Vixen* was off Cape Bon chasing a Tripolitan corsair.

As we slowly moved through the water, we had three leadsmen making soundings. When one called out that we had only seven fathoms beneath us, the captain broke off the chase and started to beat back out to sea. We didn't get far. The ship shuddered to a stop, throwing many of us right off our feet. We'd hit a reef and were now five or six feet out of the water, about three miles from Tripoli and only a mile or so offshore.

I rushed to the side and looked over. We were well and truly grounded. The ship leaned far to the port; even walking on the deck was difficult.

The ship's officers came about in a panic, ordering the sailors to and fro as they tried to get us off the rocks and sand bar. We Marines stood to the side, ready to help however we could, but trying not to get in the way of the bluejackets.

The lookout shouted, and I took my attention away from the rock and back to the harbor. The xebec had made the refuge, but from that same harbor, nine gunboats sallied forth.

The captain gave orders as he tried to free us. He crowded on sail to try and move us forward off the rocks, then laid the sails back to shift us astern. He ordered our three bow anchors cut away, and all our water heaved overboard. In desperation, he ordered the foremast cut away, and this tore off the topgallant as well when it fell.

Even with the gunboats now firing at us, he ordered most of our guns thrown overboard. With the angle of the ship, we could not depress our guns low enough to fire on the gunboats. We fired anyway, more to remind the Tripolitans that we were armed than to actually hit them. With the stern up so high, though, our quarterdeck guns, the only ones left on the ship, started a fire on the stern when they fired. Only quick work by the tars and Marines saved the ship from the flames.

By late afternoon, the situation was very dire. Captain Bainbridge called forward the ship's officers to discuss striking the colors. When we heard that, all the Marines and a good many of the ordinary seamen protested loudly, shouting that we would rather die than become slaves. But the captain, he ignored us. He was determined to save lives, he said.

We all knew the captain had struck his colors before. He was the captain of the *Retaliation* in 1798 when he surrendered to the *L'Insurgente* and *Volontaire* off Guadaloupe. It seemed to us he was now twice damned.

The captain ordered the rest of the guns thrown overboard, the magazine flooded, the hull drilled, and the signal books destroyed. We threw shot into the pumps so as the Tripolitans could not save her, then the seaman manning the ensign halyards was ordered to strike our colors. He refused, even when threatened to be run through with a sword. A midshipman had to push the seaman aside and take on the disgraceful duty himself. I don't think nary a man didn't have tears as we saw our flag come down. In the distance, we could hear the cheers from the sailors on the gunboats.

We waited as several boats moved forward, suspicious of a ruse, I'm guessing. But we had no ruse in store. We were well and truly surrendered. They still would not come closer, though. The captain sent one boat to assure them that we were done. It took some persuading, but eventually, the Class 1 Frigate *USS Philadelphia* surrendered to one gunboat.

"Come on, boys, look sharp," Mr. Osborne shouted, forming us up in ranks as the first of the Tripolitans finally reached us. "Let's show them what we are."

"What we are" were prisoners, I wanted to say. We were prisoners of the Bashaw of Tripoli.

Jonathan P. Brazee

Chapter 12

USS Enterprise
Off Tangiers

November 5, 1803

Seth

"You're not chopping wood here," Master-at-Arms Wiggins shouts, frustrated with my progress.

I knows I need "finesse," as he keeps telling me, but sometimes, I just wants to hit something. Ever since our raid, I keeps the cutlass they gives me, though I have to give back the pistols. But I wants to learn to use it like a proper gentleman. I first asked Sergeant Wren, but he doesn't use a blade much, so he asks the master-at-arms. From the petty officers, he's the best with a blade. Lieutenant Hull, mayhaps he's better, but I canst ask an officer to teach me, for sure.

So now, every other day, I gets with Seaman Hank Tuttle from Pott's Grove back in Pennsylvania, just a few miles away from me pa's farm. He's a good strong lad, and we makes a good team, not just for swordwork, but for all things. We even goes ashore together, sometime him with me and Marines, sometimes me with him and sailors.

Wiggins pulls us apart, then goes over that parry one more time. It's good to attack first, but you gots to know how to protects yourself, too. He tells us to remember our just distance, and when we are close enough to attack, so's our enemy. We step back, then gets ready to try on each other again. It's only then that I sees an officer, a lieutenant standing by watching us. We stops to see what he wants. I don't recognizes him, but as rightful as our officers are on the *Enterprise*, you needs to be careful around any officer.

Then he says, "Master-at-Arms, if I may?" with his hand out.

Wiggins steps back, then hands the lieutenant his cutlass. The lieutenant holds it, shakes it a mite to gets its feel, then takes a few lunges.

"As the master-at-arms said, you are not chopping wood. The cutlass is a heavy blade, and its forte may very well be chopping, but you need to remember, a tree does not fight back. You cannot ever forget a strong defense, and you can never forget the point of your blade. You," he says, pointing at me, "shall we take this *alla macchia?*"

He stands there waiting, but I don't know what to do. I don't know his foreign language, but I can tells he wants me to have at him. I can thwacks Hank good, and we've both got cuts and bruises to prove it, but an officer?

"I assume I must use English, private. My apologies. I want you to lunge at me."

I still hesitates. He's an officer, and striking an officer is a flogging for sure, mayhaps even a dangle from the yardarm.

"You do speak English, correct? You understand an order from a superior officer?"

An order's an order, so I step into a lunge. He just takes a step back.

"I had the impression that you had some fire. Maybe I was mistaken. Why don't you try it one more time?"

He looks prissy there, smiling at me, and I thinks I have an order, so I lunges at him, full strength. And then my hand is empty, the cutlass spinning on the deck ten feet from me. My wrist hurts fierce.

I'm not bragging, but I knows I'm strong. When we hang on the rigging to see who can stays the longest, I always win. But this lieutenant, he takes my cutlass like I was a baby. He walks over, picks it up, then comes back and hands it to me.

"Let's go over this now and see where your mistake was," he says, like nothing happened.

For the next hour, this lieutenant, the master-at-arms, Hank, and me, we drills hard. The lieutenant doesn't let up, and he even gets a good bruise from Wiggins. But he doesn't get mad, he laughs, then hits Wiggins harder the next go 'round. And he takes the time to stop and teaches me and Hank, showing us how to do each move.

Other men come to watch, even Mr. Lane and the captain. But no one else comes to join us. It is just us four.

Finally, the lieutenant wipes his brow and steps back.

Jonathan P. Brazee

"Thank you for the practice, gentlemen," he says, like me and Hank is really gentlemen. "But I'm afraid duty calls."

He goes over to where he put his jacket, then puts it back on. After he first takes it off to drill with us, it was easy to forgets he was an officer, so excited was I, but now, I remembers. He's a Navy officer.

He bows his head to us, then goes over to the captain, and shakes his hand. He goes over the side and down into a jolly boat. I walks over to the side, too, and watches his crew pull away.

"Who is that?" I ask.

"That's Lieutenant Stephen Decatur, the commanding officer of the *Argus*," one of the midshipmen answers.

The man has just laced me solid, and even my hair hurts, I thinks. But within all due respect for Mr. Lane and even our captain, I thinks that Mr. Decatur is the kind of man I would follow into hell itself.

Chapter 13

Tripoli
November 25, 1803

Ichabod

I'm not sure I was ever this hungry even at Valley Forge. How our captors expect us to work with so little food and water, I am at a loss.

When we were first taken as slaves, the officers were taken up to the old American consulate where they were fed and given leave to do what gentlemen do when they are bored. Mr. Porter, for example, had arranged for classes for the younger officers and midshipmen. But for us, those at the bottom end of the scale, we were simple slaves, made to labor mightily with little sustenance.

At first, we received some pork and beef from the *Philadelphia's* stores, but that lasted for only about two weeks. After that, each day, we were given two 12-ounce loaves of black barley bread, full of straw and chaff, three-quarters of a gill of oil, and a small amount of pork or beef every two weeks. If we were hauling stones or pushing wagons out into the desert, we didn't eat nor drink until we returned to our jail. Shoeless, shirtless, we toiled in the hot sun, feet and back burning, belly crying for food.

If William Ray thought punishment on the *Philadelphia* was his bugaboo, then now he knows what real punishment can be. Except for mayhaps David Burling, my friend who was in irons for sleeping on post and facing a dangle, but was freed when we went aground, I think most men would rather face even the fiercest wrath of one of our officers than what we faced with the Mahomatens.

On our second day as prisoners, our handlers marched a few of us, those who were not already working, out into a stone yard, where we waited in the hot sun. Finally, they dragged forward a poor wretch, a

Swede who'd been a slave for years. He was stripped naked and hoisted up over a sharpened wooden stake. His cries for pity affected us all, but we could do nothing as he was dropped on the stake, driving it up his feak and into his body as he screamed in agony.

We never found out what he did to warrant such treatment, whether it was murder, trying to escape, or just not working hard, but the lesson was obvious. The Mahomatens did it because they could. And they could do it to us as well, any time they chose.

Every night, we slept on the stone floor of our jail with only a sailcloth between our shivering bodies and the rock. Every morning, we were roused and marched off to wherever the bashaw needed work to be done. Beatings were commonplace, a part of life. Hunger was present at all times.

The *Philadelphia* had more than a few British-born crew who tried to claim British protection. They signed a petition to Lord Nelson, but as First Lieutenant John Johnson told us enlisted Marines later, Nelson responded with "If there was anything with this business, it would be to have the rascals all hung."

Our situation was dire, but even then, our patriotic feelings could not be completely suppressed. On November 8, we were told to line up in parade, and when the bashaw rode by, we were to give him three cheers. How we could do this to our captor, I cannot fathom. When the bashaw rode though our prison yard, most of us refused to cheer, but those who did, gave not a "huzzah" but brayed like an ass.

One of our tormentors was a Neapolitan. He had been a slave too, but he turned turk. He became a Mahomaten, and since one Mahomaten could not keep another as a slave, he was freed. He became one of our drivers, and a more cruel man I don't think I have seen. Turning turk could send a man high. The Tripolitan admiral, Murad Reis, was a former slave, a Scotsman by the name of Peter Lisle who had been taken off an American merchantman. He had been a slave but turned turk, even married the bashaw's daughter. He often came to observe us, and on the first day, he asked us if Captain Bainbridge was a coward or a traitor, for who else would strike the colors of a frigate of 44 guns and 300 men to a single gunboat? While he deserved all enmity for his sins, his accusations of cowardice against Captain Bainbridge found some degree of agreement amongst the crew.

We had our own turn-turk as well. John Wilson, a German quartermaster who spoke the local dialect, became a Mahomaten. He told the bashaw that Captain Bainbridge had thrown nineteen bags of dollars and gold overboard. The captain protested, and all the officers were moved to the dungeon for one night. The bashaw threatened the captain's servant with a most fierce pounding, but there were no bags of dollars. When the captain accused Wilson, he first denied it, but then put on the turban and became one of our drivers, one of the more cruel amongst them.

I must report, though, that if we white Christian slaves were mistreated, the real horror was what the black African slaves suffered under their Moorish owners. They were treated worse than dogs, and I wished upon them deliverance. Just as being a slave of the Arabs made the punishments received aboard the Navy light, so did watching the Moorish slaveholders make our own Arab masters seem genial and generous.

Our most horrible task, though, was to raise our own ship, the *Philadelphia*. Captain Bainbridge had ordered her sunk, but she hadn't gone down. A storm came up three days later, and the ship floated off the very reef what held her captive. Our masters marched us to the shore, stripped us, then forced us into the water where we had to shovel sand into baskets and carry them ashore. The water was cold, and we suffered more from that than from our masters' beatings. It was not until 2 o'clock that they permitted us to get out of the water and get a bite of bread, then it was back until sunset. Still wet from the sea, we slept on the sand. After days of such work, we were finally able to raise our ship, and it was towed back into the harbor. The knowledge that our misery only succeeded in giving the bashaw a capital ship weighed heavy on each of us.

Chapter 14

USS Enterprise
Dec 16, 1803
Malta

Seth

"Get dressed, the captain wants to see you," Sergeant Wren says, kicking my feet while I sits and mends my linens.

"What did I do?" I asks as I jumps up, reaching for my dress uniform. Linen overalls was no good when you is called before the captain.

"Don't know, but get moving," he says to me before leaving.

I rushes to get dressed, checking everything. Lieutenant Hull's a right fair man, but he's still the captain. Satisfied, I rush up the ladder, across the deck, and down to the captain's cabin. Adrian Pohl is on sentry duty, and he turns, rapping on the door to announce me.

"Private Crocker, here at the captain's orders," he says.

I tug down on the bottom of my jacket as a voice tells me to enter. I goes in and looks for Lieutenant Hull, but he's not there. It's Lieutenant Decatur, the officer who gave me a lesson in sword work; he's sitting there reading some papers.

"Uh, sir, I'm here for the captain," I says, peering around as if the captain was playing seek and hide.

"Which is reasonable, as I am the captain," he says, looking up and seeing me. "Oh, it's my young opponent, I see. You are Private Crocker, I presume?"

"Yes, sir, that be me."

"Well, I have a message for you from Private Brissey. His message is that he will meet you in the bashaw's palace and share a drink for old times."

I stands there stunned. First, that Lieutenant Decatur is in the captain's cabin, and second, that he knows Jacob. I guesses I can says third, because what officer carries messages between privates?

"You do know Private Brissey, correct?"

"Yes, sir, I does. But he's back in America now."

"Well, I think that will surprise him as I just spoke to him this morning before coming here to take command of this ship. He looked like he was on the *Argus* to me, not in America, but I suppose I could be mistaken."

"You're in command, sir?"

"I think that would be best if I'm going to occupy the captain's cabin, don't you think?"

"Uh, yes, sir, of course, sir. Um, sir, what about Lieutenant Hull?"

I likes Lieutenant Hull, and I hopes he's not in trouble, like old Commodore Morris was.

"Lieutenant Hull has taken command of the *Argus*. I am sure he will do a fine job there. But now that I've passed on the message, I am sure you have other duties?"

"Oh yes, sir, thank you, sir!" I says, getting ready to 'bout face.

"Oh, and Private Crocker? If anyone is going to meet the other in the bashaw's palace, I expect it will be crewmen from the *Enterprise* who get there first." He stands up and walks over to me clapping my shoulder hard. "If you're going to be ready to take on the Tripolitans, I want to see how far you've progressed with your cutlass. Say, 5 o'clock on the forecastle?"

I feels a surge of excitement as I says, "Yes, sir! I'll be there," before rushing out the cabin, almost running into Mr. Macdonough, who is waiting to see the new captain. I thinks interesting times are going to be ahead for us.

Jonathan P. Brazee

Chapter 15

USS Enterprise
Off Tripoli

Dec 23, 1803

Seth

With the *Philadelphia* taken, the officers canst thinks of much else but taking her back. Lieutenant Decatur seems like the commodore's right-hand man, and together, they talks about nothing else.

I hears a lot now, 'cause the captain, he calls me his bodyguard. I thinks he can take care of hisself, but I is proud that he trusts me, and my sentry post now is always outside his door. The sergeant, he tried only once to move me to another post, but when I says I will be kilt first, he backs down.

I hears how Captain Bainbridge finds a way to write the commodore, secret-like. He uses lemon juice as ink, and the commodore, he holds the letter up to a candle, and then the words can be seen. I thinks this is right clever, and I tries it myself. I gets a lemon from the mess, then uses the juice to writes my name on a piece of paper. When it dries, you canst see anything, but when you warms it up with a candle, there's my name as clear as the nose on my face.

But Commodore Preble, he wants more information about the bashaw's defenses. So he comes on the *Enterprise*, and we sails close like to the harbor, and he and Lieutenant Decatur looks through the spyglasses, discussing the bashaw's guns.

Then we sees a ketch flying British colors trying to sneak into the harbor. We gives chase and stops her. She's not British, but the Tripolitan *Mastico*. She's got a Turkish master, some Greeks and Turks, about 12 Tripolitan soldiers, and over 40 black slaves. We goes aboard to search her, and in the captain's cabin, I finds an American sword that I gives to Sergeant Wren, and he gives it to the captain.

"This is Lieutenant Porter's sword," he says with some force.

I look surprised. I fought with Lieutenant Porter, I sees him shot twice by the Mahomatens. And now, I finds his sword on a Mahomaten ship.

We goes back to the *Enterprise,* where the captain shows the commodore the sword. We knows now that this ship plundered the *Philadelphia.* The commodore claims her as a prize, and orders us to sail for Syracuse with him where he says he has plans for it.

I watches the commodore get into his jolly boat to return to the *Constitution.* I knew our captain respects him, and that counts for me, but I still feels a bit nervous around him. Everyone says he's a hard man with a real temper. He issues 106 orders on how we's suppose to act. He orders 36 lashes for Corporal Wallace, a fine Marine I knows well, when James fouls his attempt to fumigate the spaces on the ship, nots because he fails, but because he doesn't asks the commodore first.

But mayhaps Lieutenant Decatur, he knows how to handle him. When Mr. Boyd gets drunk and pounds a few locals in Syracuse two weeks ago, Mr. Lawrence and Mr. Thorn tries to get him back on the ship. Mr. Boyd draws a knife on Mr. Lawrence, but the lieutenant knocks the midshipman down to the bottom of the boat.

Mr. Boyd is a midshipman, but not the young kind. He's a big man, mayhaps 25 years old. But he's a midshipman and Mr. Lawrence is a lieutenant. We knows Commodore Preble is going to lash him proper, maybe more, but Lieutenant Decatur, he somehow talks to the commodore, and all that happens is Mr. Boyd gots to apologize to the Sicilians and to us crew.

The captain, he's a swell, a gentleman, and he treats us with a soft hand saying we will works harder for him iffen he does. But he's no cock-robin. Scuttlebutt[17] is he's a famous duelist, him and his friend Lieutenant Somers. Lots of officers duel, and some already be kilt, even a Marine captain last year. But Lieutenant Decatur, he's been in a pot load of duels, and he was Lieutenant Somers' second when he challenges six men. Somers, he gets hit on the first one, then gets hit again with the second one.

---

[17] Scuttlebutt: rumor

Jonathan P. Brazee

Now sitting on the ground, all wounded like, he has Lieutenant Decatur help him aims his pistol for the third one. I donst know if all that is true, and I donst know what happened to the other three challenges, but that's the scuttlebutt.

But I do knows that last year, young Mr. Bainbridge, a midshipman younger than me and Captain Bainbridge's own brother, gets pushed in Malta by a British nob, a famous duelist, and he has to challenge. Our captain is Mr. Bainbridge's second, and he makes them fires at two paces 'stead of ten, and the nob is so bombled that he misses his shot. The captain tells Mr. Bainbridge to go calm, and then Mr. Bainbridge shoots the nob right in his noddle[18] and kilts him dead.

We knows our captain can handles the commodore, we knows he can handles a duel, but we thinks he can handle the Turk even better. We looks forward to seeing that.

---

[18] Noddle: head

Chapter 16

USS Argus
Syracuse, Sicily

December 25, 1803

Jacob

A lovely melody filled the still night air around the *Argus* as Mr. O'Bannon played his fiddle alone on the forecastle. Our Lieutenant of Marines was never without his fiddle, and his skill in coaxing melodies out of it often had the crew enraptured.

"Happy Yuletide," I greeted the lieutenant, bringing him a cup of rum.

As an officer of Marines, he could get as much rum as he wanted, but with the captain authorizing an extra measure of rum for Christmas, I thought I would bring him a cup.

He turned to me and said, "Happy Christmas, Private Brissey. A most happy Christmas."

First Lieutenant Presley O'Bannon was a fine, impressive officer, calm of countenance and broad of shoulders. He had an inner fire, though, so while he treated his subordinates with fairness and justice, there was no doubt that he would be a terror in a battle. He was from Virginia, and his manners reflected that more genteel state.

Acting Sergeant Campbell was the Marine second-in-command, but Mister O'Bannon often used me as his orderly, given my ability to read and write tolerably well. I didn't mind the extra duties, and I rather admired the lieutenant.

I think the Lord was watching over me when I was assigned to the *Argus*. On our crossing, we had Lieutenant Decatur as our captain, and there cannot be many better officers in the American Navy. I was sad when Lieutenant Hull took command, but he was also a fine officer, and with him, morale remained high.

The ship itself was a beauty. Although almost identical to the *Vixen*, she sailed as if Neptune himself had made her. Never had a ship handled so well. Lieutenant Decatur adored her, and now Lieutenant Hull reveled in having her as his command.

I looked over the rail at Syracuse. She was lit up well with the revelries of Christmas. Most of the officers and crew were ashore, but Lieutenant O'Bannon had come back onboard early. Syracuse was a fine enough town, with cheap food and a welcoming population, but I knew that the commodore had changed his homeport to keep more sailors on board and reduce the likelihood of them deserting to joining the Royal Navy. Gibraltar and Malta offered too many opportunities for that with British captains trying to entice our men with better pay. The commodore was off to Tripoli at the moment, but we had been sent back to Syracuse for supplies.

"So what do you think, Private Brissey? Are we going to see action this coming year?"

I knew a man like the lieutenant was like a stallion, chafing at the bit. He had to be released to make his mark on history.

"I imagine so, sir. We cannot let the bashaw keep over 300 souls prisoner. Commodore Preble won't allow it. We'll have something to say about that, I'm sure."

"I trust you are correct, private; I trust you are correct."

1804

The loss of the *USS Philadelphia* had major repercussions, both militarily and politically. Back in Washington, Alexander Hamilton used the incident to attack President Jefferson's policies as failures. Jefferson, in turn, used the incident to argue for more money to be allotted for the war. A 2 ½ percent duty on imported goods was earmarked for the war effort, the first time any specific funding for the war had been identified. Six more frigates were ordered to join Commodore Preble in the Mediterranean where the enlarged squadron would be commanded by Commodore Samuel Barron.

Commodore Preble did not learn of the loss of the *Philadelphia* until November 25, 1803. He immediately considered ways to destroy the ship, both to keep her from being used against US forces as well for national pride.

Commodore Preble met Lieutenant Decatur for the first time in Gibraltar after the crossing. Immediately taken with the young officer, he, by all accounts, saw a kindred fighting spirit. Decatur quickly became a confidant of the commodore. Despite this, the commodore switched captains between the *USS Enterprise* and the *USS Argus*. Preble had helped build the *Argus* and often referred to it as "his ship," and he thought the more experienced Hull would make better use of the ship's superior handling.

In Tripoli, the Pasha reveled in the capture of the *Philadelphia* and its crew. He received offers from other Barbary states for the ship, and he started bargaining for a ransom for the crew. Life for the officers was generally acceptable. Certain officers, such as the ship's surgeon, Lieutenant Cowdery, essentially had the run of the city after treating one of the Pasha's sons. The enlisted men had it much worse. Some skilled prisoners worked in the boat yard or the foundry, but most were put to manual labor where their treatment was severe. If not for the intervention of the Danish consul, Nicholas Nissen, life would have been even worse. However, Mr. Nissen took up their cause and managed to bring in both food and money to supplement the rations they received from the Pasha.

As the year dragged on, Preble, through the intercession of Mr. Nissen, was able to get more money to the crew as well as send supply ships with food for their consumption.

. After Lieutenant Decatur's attack of February 16, Lord Nelson called it "the most daring act of the age." Pope Pius VII remarked that "the United States, though in their infancy, had done more to humble the anti-Christian barbarians on the African coast than all the European states had done for a long period of time." For the *Philadelphia* prisoners, life became immediately more severe, but slowly their treatment improved until the bombardment of August 3 began and the belief that the Americans mistreated Tripolitan sailors in the subsequent gunboat battles.

On March 7, Lieutenant Colonel Franklin Wharton became the new commandant of the Marine Corps. One of his first acts was to order a redesign of the Marine uniform, issuing the Corps' first formal uniform order on March 25.

Commodore Preble requested gunboats from the Kingdom of the Two Sicilies, which was also at war with the Tripolitans. King Ferdinand readily acceded to the request, sending six gunboats and two barges, which had to be towed from Syracuse to Tripoli, arriving at the end of July. Each gunboat had a 32-pound mortar as well as a 24-pound gun on the foredeck.

Commodore Barron, on his flagship, the *USS President*, arrived off the coast of Tripoli on September 9 and assumed command of the Mediterranean Squadron. With him was William Eaton, who was given a rank of Navy lieutenant and a new title, "Naval Agent for the Barbary Regencies."

Chapter 17

Tripoli
January 4, 1804

Ichabod

The first two of our number died in captivity. John Hilliard died on the evening of January 3 and William Anderson died on the 4th. Both men were sailors and had been sickly since we were taken. Mr. Cowdery attempted to treat them, but the cold prison and miserable conditions made their recovery nigh impossible. We put the two shipmates on cots, then took them out to the beach west of the city and gave them a Christian burial.

Without the kind intercession of Mr. Nissen, the Danish consul, I am sure more of us would have perished. Our good clothes, which had been taken by the Neapolitan slaves to be cleaned, were never returned, and the dry rags that we were at first grateful to receive became our only clothing. It struck many of us as a most cruel turn that fellow Christians would treat us so poorly.

Even amongst ourselves, we had bastards. We first took to saving one loaf of black bread at night so we could have a morsel in the morning before our labors. But thieves amongst us took this loaf more than once. The first time this happened, Mr. Morris managed to send down a loaf of good white bread, but on other times, we had to do without upon waking.

With short rations, poor clothing, a cold prison, and hard labor, many of us suffered. The bastmanding[19] we received almost daily at the hands of our drivers pushed us to the brink of survival. Yet somehow, we managed to keep breathing.

---

[19] Bastmanding: a beating

Jonathan P. Brazee

The captain tried to keep our spirits up. He sent us a message that read:

Behave like Americans, be firm, and do not despair, the time of your liberation is not far distant.   You ought not to let the threats of those into whose hands you have fallen intimidate you, but obstinately persist in your rights of being treated as prisoners and not as Slaves.

I think it was only the suggestion that our liberation was near that kept us going. Prisoners or slaves, we had no power o'er that.

Chapter 18

USS Intrepid
Tripoli Harbor
February 16, 1804

Seth

"Leave some turks for us!" Jacob shouts into a speaking trumpet as we slips by the *Argus* and out to sea on February 2.

It's been good to spends time with him as we gets my new ship ready for our mission. It would be better if Ichabod's with us, but now we knows he's in Tripoli, a prisoner of the bashaw.

We donst know exactly the mission, but with Lieutenant Decatur and Mr. Macdonough aboard and with the commodore spending so much time when we gets the ship ready, we thinks it will be good. We spends our time with powder, oil, and shot getting the *Intrepid* shipshape, then leaves with the *USS Siren*. For crew, we gots 50 sailors, 12 officers and midshipmen, eight of us Marines, and the Sicilian Salvatore Catalano, the pilot of the *Constitution*.

The next day, the captain, he tells us we's going to take back the *Philadelphia* or burn her if she's not seaworthy. All of us cheers until our throats is raw.

For four days, things is OK, but then it gets miserable. I's been at sea for nigh on three years, but the gale is fierce, and the *Intrepid* is a scow in these seas. I cascades[20] more than once, as has most the crew. I thinks when we gets to Tripoli, I will bash[21] the bashaw right on his noddle for putting us through this.

---

[20] Cascade: to vomit
[21] Bash: to hit

The *Intrepid* is the new name for our prize, the ketch *Mastico*. But a new name don' makes her seaworthy. We all work pumping and bailing to keeps her afloat, even the officers. We Marines sleep over the portside waters casks, the midshipmen and the pilot over the starboard. The sailors, they's down in the hold with the bilge water and the rats. We has rotten beef, so we's plenty hungry, and we gots no easy sleep, so we cheers when we finally see land. But in the storm, which still hollers about us, we misses our mark, and it takes us another day to make our way to Tripoli. Still, we canst do anything. Mr. Catalano takes a look, but the gale is still too fierce. The *Siren*, she tries to weigh anchor, but several crewmen gets injured, and they have to cut away the anchor. We has to follow. It takes another week 'fore we can come back.

On February 15, back at Tripoli, Lieutenant Decatur and Lieutenant Stewart meets again. They decide that we will goes forward the next day.

On the 16th, it's sunny and calm, so in the morning, flying British colors, we puts out a drag to makes it look likes we gots heavy cargo. On deck's the captain, Mr. Morris, 'bout ten sailors, and Mr. Catalano. Theys all dressed in local clothes, even the captain. I never seen him out of his uniform, and he looks mighty strange.

It takes us almost to nightfall afore we comes into the harbor. Most of us still huddles below decks, blades ready as our ship nears the *Philadelphia*. A voice cries out and we gets ready, but Mr. Catalano, he speaks the Mahomaten language, and he calls back, easy as you please. One of the sailors crouched below with us tells us that the pilot tells the crew of the *Philadelphia* that we lost our anchor, and we needs to put a line to them fors the night. He goes on 'bout the weather and our anchor as we comes up near.

We lowers a boat, and our sailors takes a line over. Then the *Philadelphia* crew hauls us tight 'longside.

Then we hears a voice shout, "Americanos!"

We don't need to hear the captain shout, "Board!" We's moving as the *Philadelphia* opens her gunports and the tampions are knocked from the guns. We rushes out screaming like Shawnee and joins Mr. Morris and the captain on the deck of the *Philadelphia*. For this attack, we has no guns, only blades, and as I sees the Tripolitans, I is glad of the lessons I takes. We rushes them.

I is excited, but I still feels a knot in my pudding. The Tripolitans, though, they back up, trying to push others to the fore. We hits them hard. One Mahomaten in front of me tries to lift his blade, but another is too close to him, and he can't raise it up. I slashes down, cutting his arm; his blade clatters to the deck. I goes to strike him again, but Mr. Morris gets in front of me and runs the man through and through. I struck the first blow, but the midshipman kilts him.

I looks for someone else to strike, but some are jumping overboard, and for the rest, there's too many Americans in my way. I slip on some blood, but I stays ready for any opportunity.

I looks at the dead sailor in front of me. My own polt[22] right near takes off his arm. I could sees white bone sticking out of the gash. Mr. Morris' blow is cleaner, but it is the one that kilts him. He looks like my age, and his peepers be open, looking at hell, I 'spect. I kilt men before, but I never sees them this close. I feels the same as when I sees a dead hog back on my pa's farm, though. God says "thou shalt not kill," but he means only for Christian folk, not Mahomatens. So I feels good about it.

Lieutenant Decatur, he fires off a rocket. This is the signal to the *Siren* that the *Philadelphia* is ours. It also tells the Tripolitans that we has taken her. The fort's cannons open up, and two corsairs near us fire their muskets as we hurry to fire the ship. Without her foremast, Lieutenant Decatur knows the ship is not seaworthy, and our little *Intrepid* canst tow her out, so he orders the ship fired. We Marines, we follow Mr. Morris to the cockpit first and then the store room and sets them afire. Each team has their own place to fire, and we gots those two places. Lieutenant Decatur, he don' wants anyone to be able to puts the fire out, so he wants the whole ship ablaze afirst, not one part that spreads to another part.

I puts more oil on the shelves of the storeroom, then uses my candle to fire it. It whooshes and I feels the heat against my face. I wants to watch it more, but Mr. Morris, he yells for us to fall back. We makes our way out to the deck, and I is amazed. The whole ship is ablaze. I feel like I is in an oven, cooking like. Flames shoot out of the portholes as other sailors scurry out for safety, like rats fleeing a burning building. We all is dirty and smoke-faced, but our smiles is big.

---

[22] Polt: a blow, particularly a strong blow

Jonathan P. Brazee

The officers is yelling at us to get back on the *Intrepid*, which that crew has cut away so as it does not catch afire, too. I jumps as our valiant ship moves away, just clearing the rail and onto the deck. I looks back, and only Lieutenant Decatur is still on board, looking like a god with the flames around. He stands there another moment, like he's admiring our work, then turns and jumps into the rigging of the *Intrepid*.

Our little *Intrepid* has no sail furled, so two boats is towing us. We puts out the sweeps to join in, and slowly, we makes our way out of the harbor. None of us, though, can keeps our eyes off the *Philadelphia*. She burns so bright. We don't cheers, though, just sits in silence. I thinks some things are so glorious, we needs no words.

Chapter 19

Tripoli
April 24, 1804

Ichabod

John Morisson died today.

We were loading timber outside of the city three days ago. Trying to get one of the logs onto the cart, we dropped it, and John was crushed. We carried him back to the prison and called for Mr. Cowdery or Dr. Ridgby, but instead, Blinkard, we called him, our Algerine driver who fancied himself a doctor, came with Lewis Hexiner, one of our crew who had turned turk and put on the turban.

Blinkard examined the poor tar, then declared him a *romo kelp*, or infidel dog, as well as a slacker and a laggard, and beat him soundly with his bamboo. Blinkard was a cruel man, ferocious in his treatment of us. And with the fleet offshore, the Turks treated us more cruelly, as they did when Lieutenant Decatur burned the *Philadelphia* to the waterline. But this was too much, and we cursed his name. John died the next morning despite Blinkard's claim he was merely a slackard.

Blinkard was only one of our cruel drivers. The head was a Moor named Abdallah, or Captain Blackbeard, as we called him. He was a quiet and cunning man. He never deigned to scream and shout, but his punishments were none the lighter for that.

We called Soliman "Scampin Jack." He was Tunisian, an evil man, a true hector.[23] Like other bullies, he took every opportunity to show his power over us.

---

[23] Hector: a bully

Joseph was a Frenchman, the chief steward of the ex-bashaw. Like many men who feel they have to prove themselves, he was more apt to strike us at the least provocation.

Red Jacket was a Tripolitan, and our shelling killed his wife. We thought he wanted an opportunity to kill some of us, so we remained very wary when he was around.

Only Bandy treated us with any degree of compassion. We called him Bandy 'cause of his bandy legs. He was a Greek, a Mameluke of the ex-bashaw, but unlike Joseph, he seemed to sympathize with our plight. We all wanted to be on his work detail each day, and he seemed to enjoy the esteem we placed on him.

We buried John alongside his shipmates outside of town, wondering when we would be delivered from bondage. Just off shore, we could see American ships, but they might as well have been back in Baltimore for all they could do for us.

Chapter 20

USS Argus
Off Tripoli
July 17, 1804

Jacob

Commodore Preble was on board again, something he was oft wont to do. He helped build this ship, and he liked to come aboard. We were making a reconnaissance, and the commodore and Lieutenant Hull were glassing the harbor yet one more time.

The *Argus* was perhaps the best handling ship of the squadron, so lately, the commodore had us making quick forays into the harbor to draw fire and have the Tripolitans reveal their positions. I wasn't so sure I liked being a decoy for the fort's guns, but I was only a private of Marines, to be seen and not heard.

I looked over at Lieutenant O'Bannon, who was standing silently with the ship's first lieutenant as they listened in. I knew he ached for action. When we learned about Decatur's daring raid to burn the *Philadelphia*, he had been struck by a strange melancholy, not because the *Philadelphia* burned, for he exulted over that, but because he hadn't taken part in that glorious action.

He confided to me later that our missions of being a courier and now the commodore's pleasure launch frustrated him to no end. He wanted us to have an opportunity to show our true colors as fighting men.

As usual, the Tripolitans fired shots to keep us at a distance. We had moved in closer, but neither the captain nor the commodore seemed concerned. The fort fired once more, and a few moments later, a shot crashed into the ship, right below where the commodore was standing.

The shot tore off our copper and holed our hull. Commodore Preble leaned over the rail to see the damage, then calmly asked Lieutenant Hull to remove us from the harbor. It seemed that this day's pleasure cruise was over.

Chapter 21

The Mediterranean Squadron Gunboats
Tripoli Harbor
August 3, 1804

Seth

"Back into the fray we go," Sergeant Wren says as we prepares ourselves.

We is a good crew now, sailors and Marines. We has a good captain, and we trusts him through thick and thin. 'Cause of him, the scuttlebutt is that the whole ship is going to get two months extra pay as a bonus for burning the *Philadelphia*. That's even betters than what we gets with Lieutenant Sterett. When the captain asks for volunteers for the next attack, every Marine and nigh near every sailor volunteers.

I gets picked along with Sergeant Wren and one other Marine from the ship. Lieutenant Decatur, he says he canst do without his bodyguard, meaning me. We gots some sailors, including Hank. The captain's gunboat, it's all *Enterprise* men. The other boats, they is from the other ships. I wonders if Jacob will be there, too. His *Argus* is off Tripoli along with nigh on five other ships, including the big frigate, the *Constitution*.

We climbs down the net and into our gunboat. She's a big, slow girl, but I ˙spect she'll do. Ashore, we can see the Tripolitans gathered. Admiral Reis, the Scotsman who turned turk, gots nine gunboats of his own, and we don't thinks he'll hold back.

We is a fierce-looking crew. We has no muskets, but we has pistols, cutlasses, pikes and even tomahawks.

We is put into two divisions. We is the second division, and our boat is Number 4. With us is Mr. Bainbridge, the same one who fights the duel in Malta at two paces and whose brother is held prisoner not a mile away, and Mr. Trippe from the *Vixen*. The other division is led by Mr.

Somers, and with him is our captain's brother, James Decatur, and Mr. Blake.

We sails off to meet the Tripoltans who sally forth, too. We come under heavy musket and grapeshot fire. We fire our 24-pounder, and I thinks we strike true 'cause two Tripolitans break off and strike for the reef and safety. Sometimes in a tussle, I don't hears much else, but I hears an explosion above us. One of our two-bomb ketches has hit Molehead Battery above us.

Now, Lieutenant Decatur has sights on a full sixteen Tripolitans anchored to the leeward. We fire canister and grapeshot, raking them. Most of them cuts their mooring lines to slide back in the harbor, but in front of us were 11 more ships.

I looks around, and it seems likes all gunboats are following us, 'cepting Mr. Somers' boat. We keep closing, firing a boarding dose into the enemy. Mr. Bainbridge, in boat 5, his lateen yard is shot clean away, and he can't close. He gives fire, but only our two boats sails on to close with two of the Tripolitans.

Mr. Trippe's boat closes first, and I can sees him and his men jumps aboard the Tripolitan. Then the two boats comes apart, and he's on the enemy boat, with only 10 souls, facing what looks to be 35 Mahomatens.

But I canst watch long. We comes up to the second boat and jumps aboard her. We have 19 men; they have mayhaps 36. I donst think they 'spected us to board 'cause they cower in the back of the boat. I rushed to the fore, the first one to draw blood when I parry a saber and thrust home. The Tripolitan, he donst even act like he wants to fight, his face askeerd until I take his life. Pulling my cutlass back, I bring it up, exposing my chest, but no one takes it, and I come down like a bear, cutting another sailor's head in two. My cutlass gets stuck in the man's noddle, and I canst get it out. But around me's the rest of my crew, and they's deep into the tussle. One of the Mahomaten tries to skewer me with a pike, but I just pulls it by me and then bastes him in the mug with my fist. He goes down like a fish before Hank lambastes him, sending him on to hell.

Sudden like, it's over. None of us is wounded, but there's sixteen kilt Mahomaten, fifteen wounded, and five captured. I is breathing hard, but with the glory of victory.

We looks for another enemy, when Boat Number 2 comes alongside. I donst see Mr. Decatur, but Mr. Brown, a midshipman, shouts over that a

Tripolitan boat surrendered, but when they went to takes her, it was a ruse, and the Tripolitan captain shoots Mr. Decatur in the noddle, and he falls into the water betwixt the two boats. Mr. Brown, he fishes Mr. Decatur out of the water, but the Mahomaten boat escapes while he does that. The captain's brother is alive, but not for long.

We all goes quiet like, looking at the captain. He is stunned for only a moment, then we sees anger takes over. He shouts for Mr. Thorn to stay on the prize, and he jumps back to Boat Number 4. I follows, along with Mr. Macdonough, Sergeant Wren, and six tars. He sees a boat behind the rocks and shouts to us, "That boat killed my brother!"

We pulls for the boat with all our might and closes. There's 24 of them on board, but for the ten of us, we donst care. We fall into them like the devil hisself. I is the third man aboard, and I tries to stay near the captain, but an old greybeard comes up to meet me, cutlass in hand. He is smaller than me and older, so I thinks he is no great fighter. I raise my cutlass to bring it down on his bald pate, but with a quick flicks of his wrist, he parries me, and I is extended, my side open to him. I canst bring my blade around afore he can, and I knows he will stick me.

The captain, he spent hours with me on my swordplay, and I forgets it all, trying to use my cutlass as an axe. And now, I is open to this old Mahomaten. Just then, I remembers the lessons, where the captain tells us that the whole sword is a weapon, not only the edge. I canst bring my blade around, but the pommel is hard, and I gots muscle to use it. I bring my right hand up inside of his, holding the pommel as I baste his jowl with all my might just as he begins to slash me. Instead of feeding me cold steel, his eyes roll back and he falls. I donst thinks he is kilt, but he is out.

I step over him and rush forward, looking for the captain. He is closing with the Mahomaten captain, a giant over two yards tall. The giant swings his pike at the captain, and the captain parries it, but his cutlass snaps, and the pike pierces his chest. I shouts out and tries to go to him, but another Mahomaten meets me with two daggers, slowing me.

I takes off one of my enemy's hands above the wrist, but the man doesn't stop his tussle with me. I looks over him to see the lieutenant grabs the pike and pulls it out of his chest, then takes the Turk by the throat. They both falls to the ground, fighting. I send my blade into my own opponent's side, and it sticks to his ribs. I tries to pry it free when I sees another Mahomaten rush up, scimitar over his head to strike down our captain. I lunges forward, but I is too far away. I canst stop it. My pistols is already spent from before, and I have only my dirk now.

Lieutenant Decatur, he's on top of the Mahomaten captain, so he canst see his doom. Just as the Mahomaten sailor starts to bring his scimitar down, Dan Frasier, a tar, throws himself in front of the blade, taking it on his own noddle. I can sees his is wounded in his arms from afore, but now his noddle is cut bad, too, and I thinks he is kilt saving the lieutenant.

Afore the Mahomaten sailor can raise his scimitar again, he is shot down by another American tar. Lieutenant Decatur, he is still struggling with the Turk who, being stronger, has rolled over on top of him and pulls out his *yataghan* to slash down on the captain. I rushes forward to help, but the captain, he holds the Turk's dagger hand and pulls out his own pistol. He holds it against the Turk's back and shoots him dead.

With their captain dead, the fight's gone out of the Mahomatens, and they surrenders. Only three's not wounded. Twenty-one is kilt or hurt. For the Americans, the lieutenant's wounded, and so's Sergeant Wren and Dan Frasier. Dan's hurt mighty grievous, but he's still alive.

Over our heads, the *Constitution*'s been bombing the city, but now, she turns all guns to 'bout seven boats who is coming out to meet us. The grapeshot tears fierce into them, though, and they has to retreats.

We makes our way back to Boat Number 4, and the captain, he goes on board to hold his brother. I catches the eye of one of the sailors on board, but he shakes his head. James Decatur's dead. It isn't until a mite later when the commodore gives us the signal to retire that we returns to the *Constitution*. I follow the captain on deck when the commodore comes, his uniform all blown apart from some Mahomaten cannon shot. He asks the captain how many prizes he took, and the captain tells him three.

Commodore Preble, he shakes Lieutenant Decatur, angry like, and asks, "Aye sir, why did you not bring me more?" afore he storms off.

Lieutenant Decatur, he looks angry, and others hold him back. I is angry too, and I wants to bash the commodore, even iffen that will gets me a dangle from the yardarm. A bit later, though, mayhaps someone tells the commodore about the captain's brother, 'cause he calls him to his cabin. I stays close, but when the hatch opens, the commodore has his hands on his shoulders, and Lieutenant Decatur, he has tears in his eyes.

The commodore calls for the captain's brother to be brought to the ship, and the captain, he sits up with his brother's body all night. When we buries his brother at sea the next day, though, he is proud, not sad. He tells us he would rather have his brother in the embrace of the ocean than "living with any cloud on his conduct."

For this fight, we captures three gunboats, thirty-five prisoners, and kilt forty-seven of them, forty-four in the tussle itself. We donst know how many the *Constitution* kilt with her big guns. We had one kilt, one grievously wounded, and 'bout six or seven less wounded. Lieutenant Trippe, he takes 11 sword slashes, but he's back fighting in a couple of days. I hears that Sergeant Meredith kilt a Mahomaten with his bayonet afore that sailor could cut down Mr. Trippe. Charles Young, who I mets a few times, got his arm shattered by a cannon ball, but all says he fought on.

A few days later, the *Samuel Adams* arrives. Aside that more frigates is coming and we is getting a new commodore, we finds out that Lieutenant Stephen Decatur is promoted to captain, the youngest in the Navy.

Chapter 22

USS Argus
Off Tripoli

September 13, 1804

Jacob

Finally it looks like the crew of the *Argus* might get meaningfully involved in the war. Commodore Barron has given us a secret mission, along with Lieutenant William Eaton, to help put Hamet Qaramanli, the bashaw's exiled older brother, on the throne, making the Tripolitan beholden to the United States.

The last few months have been frustrating. While others gather glory, we sit off and fire our cannons, nary taking a shot back in return. Seth has been in three major battles, earning accolades and three months extra pay, while I have done nothing a Marine is trained to do except stand sentry duty. I have not fired once from the tops, nor gone into any attack. I helped man one of the 24-pounders Commodore Preble sent over, but that has been the entirety of my action.

We cheered Decatur's victory over the gunboats and cried over his brother's untimely death. We were saddened when we heard that Sergeant Jonathan Meredith, the Marine who saved Mr. Trippe's life not four days before, and Nathaniel Holmes, a fun-loving young private, were killed when Gunboat #9 took a direct hit from a Tripolitan shore battery. We were stunned when the doughty *Intrepid*, with Lieutenant Somers and twelve other brave souls, exploded in a huge fireball. The ship, which served so ably in firing the *Philadelphia*, was outfitted as a fireship, much as Lord Nelson had so ably done at Copenhagen, but either by Turkish shot or, as some contend, by the hand of Somers himself to avoid capture, was destroyed with all hands.

Yet we, with the nimblest ship in the Navy, sat on the action's periphery when we were not acting as a mail ship, bringing the commodore's messages back and forth. I understand my own mortality, and I long for Suva's sweet embrace, but I am still a man, and I desire to face my baptism of fire.

The situation has changed with the arrival of Lieutenant Eaton. The former consul to Tunis, he was fluent in four Arabic dialects, French, Greek, Latin, and four native Indian languages. He was an expert in the politics of the region, but more importantly, he was a fighter, not one to bow before the Turks. On board the *Argus*, he impressed us all with his marksmanship, and more spectacularly, with his ability to hit a target with a knife at 80 feet. He was an expert with the scimitar and could twirl it above his head as ably as the most skilled janissary.

A native of Connecticut, he served as a sergeant in the Continental Army, then as a captain in the Legion. He was broad across the shoulder, looking more like a brawler than a fine gentleman, although he was in fact a scholar of note. His blue eyes showed a fierce will not normally found amongst other men.

From all accounts, Commodore Barron was not enamored with him, and his support of Eaton's mission was mild. But with Captain Preble's vocal support, the commodore gave his approval. Lieutenant Eaton would not get the 100 Marines he requested, but he would get the *Argus* and her crew.

Lieutenant O'Bannon was immediately taken by the brash Eaton. He had met Eaton before in Gibraltar, and after further consultation with the man over his plan, his opinion of him only rose.

Lieutenant Eaton met with our new commandant, Lieutenant Colonel Wharton, before departing Washington. After their meetings, the commandant gave him fifty of our new uniforms. They had to be fitted to us, but we would be the only Marine unit in the squadron to be dressed out so.

The jacket was navy blue, single-breasted with naval buttons. Each button had a yellow worsted binding, going across the chest in a V-shape, with the bottom of the V at the button. We had white pantaloons with black cloth gaiters. Our new hats were something to behold. They were high and brimless, with a red plume on the side, a brass eagle cap plate, and a hat band of blue, gold, and red. The finishing touch was a tassel in the same colors.

If we thought this made us stand out, Lieutenant O'Bannon's new uniform, with a double row of eight buttons and gold bindings, red sash, red collar with more gold bindings, and knee-high boots might make Lord Nelson look on with envy. He cut quite a dashing figure.

All of us loved the new look. If we were finally going to see some action, at least we would look bounce as we entered the fray.

Chapter 23

Tripoli
September 28, 1804

Ichabod

The first blow on my feet took my breath away as the fire lanced up my body. The second opened my mouth as I cried out despite my fervent intention not to give our drivers the satisfaction.

We had seen cruel punishment before. I had watched a Swedish slave impaled, and we had all seen Berbers getting their right hand and left foot cut off before being left to die in the desert. We watched two huge Negroes accused of murder being slowly hung. But that was to others, and this was to me. I had no way to understand the agony of the bastinadoes until it was done to me.

Each blow was fire coursing from my feet to my brain. After three blows, I was in agony. After 20, I was in another place of fire, pain, and endless misery. I could not count the blows, so I could not know when my torture would end.

Two days afore, I was returning from the boatyard when three cup-shot sailors were arguing. Each week, we received a small pittance from Mr. Nissen, and most of that was used for vegetables or mayhaps a bit of beef to supplement our food. But some men would buy the liquor made from the date tree. What with the bombs our fleet had dropped on the city since August, beatings and bashings were more frequent, so me and Achilles, along with three other tars, tried to walk around the sailors, leaving them to their own devices.

It was too late, though. John Wilson, our first to wear the turban, came rushing up. Like all others, I despised the man and considered him a traitor. But he had power o'er us.

Wilson lambasted the three men, calling them infidels and more in the language of the Arab. Achilles stopped to watch, and Wilson, seeing that, became enraged. He rushed over and gave Achilles a bash on the noddle, felling him to the stone road. He started kicking him, and that was when I was o'ercome. All the last year hit me, all our suffering, all our piteous existence. I took two steps to the traitor, wheeled him about, and gave him a clout so hard he fell senseless. I may be older than most of the others, and I may not be the biggest bull in the pen, but I know how to bash, and bash I did.

Achilles stood up and looked at the man before rearing back and delivering a mighty kick to his belly. The three sailors joined in as well. Now a gentleman would not deliver a blow to a fallen foe. Unfortunately for Mr. Wilson, I was not a gentleman. I was a private of Marines, and I too, gave the man bashes of my own.

We left him on the street, alive, but in pain. When he recovered enough to return, he came into our prison crying for revenge. I could see the fear in Achilles' eyes, but as I was the only one who the bastard actually saw strike him, I boldly told him I was the only one who had done him ill. He went to the bashaw, we presume, and I was sentenced to the 500 bastinadoes.

When it was time for my punishment, with chains around my hands, I was dragged roughly by two Tripolitans and pushed down on my face. I was held there while I was beat soundly on my bumfiddle for 250 strokes. This brought tears to my eyes, and I was in agony, but this was only a hint on what was to come. When they turned me to my back, I looked up at crewmates to show them I was strong. My backside was pulsing and aching fiercely, but I thought I had acquitted myself well. When on my back, they tied my ankles to a stout piece of wood. With that, they lifted my feet up to expose them to my tormentor.

I had promised myself that no cry would escape my lips, but that did not last past the first blow. I was crying like a newborn babe. This was not the pain of them beating my pratts[24]—this was absolute agony. I couldn't breathe, I couldn't think. With each blow, lights danced in front of my eyes. I think my mind finally left me, else I could not survive the bashing. I was not aware when it ended, only that my body ached. My

---

[24] Pratts: the buttocks

crewmates came to release me from the bindings as I whimpered in shame and pain.

William Ray brought me some food and water, but I couldn't eat nor drink. How I was going to be able to walk to my work party the next day, I did not know. All I wanted was to fade away into sleep where my trials could not follow me.

Chapter 24

USS Argus
Alexandria, Egypt
November 25, 1804

Jacob

We sailed into Alexandria, the first American warship ever to do so. We fired a rousing 17-gun salute, Marines standing proud in our new uniforms that we had altered to fit in Malta. I looked at the city in awe, the very history wafting through the air. This city had existed at this very place for 2,126 years. Our own nation was only 28 years old. Two of the wonders of the world, the lighthouse and the great library, had existed here, although neither had survived the ravages of time.

We had two missions in Alexandria. Our written orders were to escort merchantmen and to let the crew take liberty. Our secret orders were to find Hamet Qaramanli and bring him back to the throne of Tripoli.

Most of the crew were not told about the secret orders. They were told to take liberty, to enjoy the exotic port of Alexandria. One small group would make contact with bashaw's elder brother.

I was one of those few men who knew our mission. Mr. O'Bannon insisted that I could be of help to the small gang.

Leading us was Mr. Eaton. He had been advocating such a mission for nigh on two years, even meeting with President Jefferson to make his case. Commodore Barron was reticent to give Mr. Eaton any support, but with Commodore Preble pushing for the mission, and then with Commodore Barron taking sick and likely to die, he finally gave Mr. Eaton the *Argus* and those of us on board who could help.

With us would be Mr. Richard Farquhar, a Scotsman who had continually pushed his service as the point of contact between the United States and the prince. He caught Commodore Preble's ear in Malta and managed to get assigned to our group. Neither Mr. O'Bannon nor I thought his intentions were honorable but rather that of a profiteer. The decision to include him, though, was up to neither of us.

Our first action in the fabled land was to pay our respects to the British consul, Mr. Biggs, and give him a letter Mr. Eaton had finagled out of Mr. Ball, the governor of Malta, asking Mr. Biggs for all the assistance he could give us. With the Turks controlling Alexandria and the surrounding Egyptian territory, we needed English support to move about freely. The next day, Mr. Biggs arranged for a meeting with the governor of Alexandria and a Turkish admiral.

At this reception, Mr. Eaton discovered that the prince, having chosen poorly in picking the Mamelukes over the Turks in Egypt, was well to the south, hundreds of miles south of Cairo. From what Lieutenant O'Bannon told me, most present at the reception advised Mr. Eaton to give up his quest.

The hinterlands of Egypt were controlled by Turkish and Albanian deserters who had formed into small armies, several rival Mameluke armies, mercenaries under the command of Mohammed Ali, Bedouin raiders, and British and French roaming groups left behind in their most recent fighting. But Mr. Eaton was not deterred.

Prevailing upon Captain Hull, he was able to get us Marines assigned to him as well as Lieutenant Joshua Blake and two midshipmen, George Washington Mann and Elis Danielson, Mr. Eaton's own stepson. Mr. Eaton also took Mr. Farquhar, the janissary Sied Selim, and a local man by the name of Ali.

Our pretense was that we were a tourist party anxious to see the sights of ancient Egypt. The sight we wanted to see, though, had nothing to do with the ancient ruins, but of one specific Tripolitan.

Jonathan P. Brazee

Chapter 25

Tripoli
December 25, 1804

Ichabod

I took a bite out of the meat, juices running out my chops and down my face. I don't know if it was mutton or camel, only that I never have tasted such heavenly fare. I shuddered to think that it almost never happened.

It had been two months with nary a bite of meat for most of us. After the bombardment, our drivers treated us in a manner not to be envied. We were told that the bashaw ordered his drivers to abuse us so that when we wrote letters, which the bashaw encouraged, we would complain so much that President Jefferson could not help but grant us deliverance.

With us so down, we petitioned Captain Bainbridge for an advance on our wages so we could have a glorious Christmas dinner. The bashaw agreed to the dinner and to make it a day with no labor, and Mr. Nissen agreed to set up the particulars. We would have meat, fresh vegetables, two loaves of white bread a man, and a quart of wine each. I dare say we dreamt of the moment for days in advance.

On Christmas morn, we woke with anticipation. To our dismay, though, our drivers came in and demanded to know who had stolen line and supplies from the boat yard. We were told that no dinner would be served until the lifter came clean. Our dreams were dashed.

Later that evening, to our great surprise, our drivers came back. Captain Blackbeard told us that the lines and supplies had been found in a Tunisian warehouse. The owner had bought them from Selim, the bashaw's brother-in-law.

Better late than never, our food soon arrived. I needed the meat, the glorious meat, but others went for the wine first. Soon, most of us were cup-shot, full in the belly and in a most happy situation. Before long, singing broke out, as we poured out our very hearts. After singing "Adieu, Blest Liberty," I 'spect not a dry eye was amongst us:

In helpless servitude forlorn
From country, friends and freedom torn,
Alike we dread each night and morn,
For naught be grief we see;
When burdens press—the lash we bear,
And all around is bleak despair,
We breath the silent, fervent prayer,
O come, blest Liberty!

And when invading cannons roar,
And life and blood from hundreds pour,
And mangled bodies wash ashore,
And ruins strew to sea;
The thoughts of death or freedom near
Create alternate hope and fear!
When will that blest day appear,
That brings sweet Liberty?

Jonathan P. Brazee

1805

As the new year began, Commodore Barron was still in Malta suffering from a liver condition. Captain Rogers had ceased the bombardment of Tripoli, but the ships of the squadron still patrolled the Mediterranean.

In Egypt, William Eaton and Lieutenant Hull were attempting to contact Hamet Qaramanli, the pasha's older brother, in an attempt at regime change. The older Qaramanli had joined forces with Arab Mamelukes, who were intent on pushing out the Turkish forces that controlled Cairo, Alexandria, and most of the coastal areas of Egypt.

After finally making contact with elder Qaramanli brother, Eaton organized a diverse army of US Marines with mercenaries from Greece, the Levant, Sicily, and northern Africa with the mission to forcibly remove the pasha and replace him with his older brother.

Commodore Preble returned to the United States in February to the adulation of the general public. Support for the war effort was extremely high.

Lieutenant Colonel William Ward Burroughs, the second commandant of the Marines, died in Washington, DC, on March 6. *The Daily National Intelligencer* of March 15, 1805, published the following:

Departed this life on the 6th instant, in the 47th year of his age, Colonel W. W. BURROWS, a Revolutionary officer, and late Commandant of the Marine Corps. The most benevolent of men, he had devoted himself to the benefit of his fellow creatures; but that malignant fiend ingratitude was his reward. After struggling with severe illness and too feeling a heart, he resigned existence with the celestial calmness of a good man.

Tobias Lear, the Consul General to the Barbary States, but residing in Malta, decided the time was ripe for a negotiated peace with Tripoli. On March 28, he sent a letter to Yusef Pasha via the Maltese Spanish counsel,

Don Gerando Joseph de Souza, accepting the pasha's premise, sent in a letter in December 1804, that an honorable peace could be had.

On May 15, Captain John Rodgers formally took command of the Mediterranean Squadron from the ailing Commodore Barron.

Chapter 26

Alexandria
February 7, 1805

Jacob

So this was the great Hamet Qaramanli, the rightful ruler of the Tripolitan throne, the very man with whom we were siding to end the war? To say I was disappointed would be a vast understatement.

Hamet Qaramanli, while not thin, was a slight man with bad skin. Nervous and wary, yet he greeted Mr. Eaton warmly as they conversed in Italian and Arabic. I knew he was 39 years old, but he seemed a man in his 50s. Effeminate in nature, he reportedly took pleasure in a never-ending supply of Turkish sweetmeats as well as in both the young women and men in his entourage.

It was not surprising that he had been deposed by his younger brother, the bashaw. From all accounts, his brother was a forceful, imposing figure. This man had killed his oldest brother, the heir to the throne, had him cut to pieces and emasculated, then had his father request permission to have him named heir over the older Qaramanli.

Hamet had been sent to Derne as a provincial governor, but he endeared no one with his manner and lack of fortitude. After trying to foment a revolt, he had to flee Derne for his very life.

Finding Hamet had been a Herculean task in and of itself. We had left Alexandria by two chartered *marches*, a type of local schooner used for river trips, on December 4, on our supposed tourist trip, making our way to the Nile. This coincided with the start of Ramadan, the month in which good Mahomaten refrained from eating and drinking from sunrise to sunset. On the second day, while waiting for the tide to allow us into the river, we debarked at Rosetta where the French and British fought their savage battle in 1801. We walked the beach still littered with the bleached bones of soldiers, a ghastly reminder of the cost of war and how combatants are so soon forgotten.

Entering the Nile, the cool blue of the Mediterranean changed to the muddy brown of the river. This was symbolic of the poor villages along the river's banks, where Turks, "wild Arabs," as Mr. Eaton referred to them, and Albanians ravaged them. When we reached the village of Sabour, a band of Arab raiders were driving off the remaining goats and sheep of the village. The day before, the village had been plundered by 500 Albanian deserters.

At Sabour, the villagers rejoiced to see us, our hats immediately identifying us as "Non-French." They kissed our hands and prostrated themselves on the ground. At first, they thought us British, but when we told them we were Americans, they wanted to know when the British would come back to restore order. They told us the British paid for everything they took; the French just took and paid for nothing.

Mr. Eaton had dressed himself in a uniform, probably his old Army uniform, and took to calling himself "General Eaton" to those whom we met. He had a flair, to be sure. He carried a rifle, not a musket, and in Sabour he placed an orange at 25 paces. With his rifle, he drilled it not once but three successive times, to the delight of the people. I thought back to Seth's arguments of keeping a rifle in preference to our Charlevilles back in Washington so long ago, and watching Mr. Eaton, I realized that Seth might have had a valid position on the matter.

We reached Cairo without incident, but in the Turkish-ruled city, how were we to find Hamet, given that he had joined with the Mamelukes? Despite our seeking to meet with one of his enemies, the viceroy treated us royally. He invited us to meet with him and offered the officers cold sherbet, coffee, and good pipe tobacco. Other than Lieutenant O'Bannon, none of the rest of the Marines were offered any of the refreshments. The sherbet looked especially delicious, and I was sore disappointed that I was not able to taste it.

Mr. Eaton was masterful in his conduct. He controlled the conversation during which he drew parallels between the United States and the Ottomans, even between Mahomatens and the particular offshoot of Christianity that we Americans practiced, seeing that we worshiped the same one God. I wasn't sure how that would be accepted back in the United States, but it seemed to give the viceroy pause.

When they finally got to the subject of Hamet, the viceroy said he had intended to assist him until prince had elected to join with the Mamelukes. Mr. Eaton told him that "it was more like God to pardon than to punish his repenting enemy," and with flowery turns of the tongue like this, we received the viceroy's promise to send emissaries to locate Hamet and then permit him to leave with us for Tripoli. I hold true, though, that the monetary gift Mr. Eaton had given the viceroy had much to do with that, despite Mr. Eaton's public protestations to the contrary.

It didn't take long for the viceroy to locate Hamet. He was in the Upper Egyptian city of Minyeh, where 3,000 Mamelukes were being besieged by 8,000 Levants and Albanians under Turkish command. The next day, on December 17, Mr. Eaton sent four messengers, three of them Maltese disguised as Arabs, to find Hamet and give him Mr. Eaton's message as well as a copy of the viceroy's pardon.

Then we sat and waited. Lieutenant Hull sent regular missives asking for progress reports. Mr. Eaton would reply that things were going well, but I could see the concern on his face. With too much nervous energy, we actually did fulfill our role as tourists. We saw the Nilometer, from which the Egyptians could ascertain the next year's bounty when they read the depth of the river during a huge festival. We went to Giza, from where we could see the famous pyramids of the Pharaohs. James Owens, another private in our group, and Acting Sergeant Campbell and I had petitioned Lieutenant O'Bannon to be allowed to go see them up close, but with Bedouins between us, Mr. Eaton would not give us permission. Even from a distance, though, I was awed to see the largest structures ever produced by man.

Mr. Eaton was not impressed with anything we saw. He said the pyramids were monuments to superstition, built under the groans of countless thousands of slaves. Even the River Nile failed to impress him. He praised the Hudson, Connecticut, Delaware, and other American rivers as being superior to the mighty Nile.

While we were waiting for Hamet's reply, Mr. Eaton had a problem with Mr. Goldborough, the *Argus'* purser. Mr. Goldborough had come ashore December 29 to deliver a message from Lieutenant Hull, and while waiting for a reply, he got into a fisticuffs with Mr. Farquhar over an argument while playing billiards. He had to be rescued by Selim from Mr. Farquhar's intention to beat him senseless. From there, the drunken purser wandered the streets of Cairo, lifting the veils of the local women. He was accused of cheating at cards, and to make matters worse, he was also accused of bilking a courtesan of her wages after visiting her at a brothel.

Mr. Eaton was livid that the locals would witness this type of behavior from an American officer, and he ordered the lieutenant back to Alexandria and to the ship. I can say this of Mr. Eaton. Along with Lieutenant O'Bannon, he looked down upon the wanton pleasures that so many sailors and Marines relished. When we were presented with belly dancers or courtesans, he refused all offers of a carnal nature.

We gathered more men to our mission as we waited in Cairo. One of the more interesting was Gervasio Santuari, also known as Lieutenant Leitensdorfer, or as he simply asked to be called, Jean Eugene. He was 36 years old, of medium height and powerful build. He claimed service in the armies of France, Austria, and the Ottomans, having deserted all three. He was Tyrolian-born, but had little allegiance to his native country. He had been a Capuchin monk and a Dervish, having publicly circumcised himself. He married a Coptic woman, then wandered the region under the name Murat Aga. He claimed to have cured the Bashaw of Trebizond of blindness, for which he collected a fine reward. He then went on a pilgrimage to Mecca and ended up in Egypt after serving as an interpreter for Lord Gordon, a Scottish peer. I have no idea how much of what he told us was the truth, but he was certainly entertaining.

On January 9, we finally received word from Hamet. He agreed with the plan to put him back on the throne and was on his way to meet us. The Maltese messenger who had delivered the message to him had first been arrested as a Turkish spy by the Mamelukes. But by the simple expediency of giving his guards spirits, he waited until they were in a cup-shot stupor, then walked out of his imprisonment and found Hamet.

While Hamet was making his way north, we took our leave of the viceroy, but not before he gave each officer a fine saber. We left Cairo and marched north to Alexandria where an eager Lieutenant Hull awaited our return. We spent the next several days procuring supplies, although the horses we bought were poor examples of the species. On January 22, Mr. Eaton left with Mr. Mann and Mr. Blake, two of the *Argus'* midshipmen, and 23 Christian recruits to meet Hamet in the village of Fayyum.

Two days later, about 75 miles from Alexandria, they were stopped by a detachment of about 500 Albanian soldiers and arrested by their commanding officer, the Kourchief. The Kourchief insisted that he would assist Mr. Eaton in finding Hamet Bashaw, but he kept Mr. Eaton and the two midshipmen, along with their servants, as prisoners, feting them with food, yet keeping them prisoner.

When the 23 recruits returned without Mr. Eaton, we considered an expedition to rescue him, but his letters advised us to remain calm. He also requested money from Lieutenant Hull, not only for Hamet Bashaw when he arrived, but as a *docuer*, or bribe for the Kourchief to ensure their release.

Mr. Mann later told Lieutenant O'Bannon, who then told me, that while a "guest" of the Kourchief, the commander had ordered the beheading of 60 peasants for not paying taxes, and hung a 12-year-old boy because his father, a village chief, could not pay his levy.

On February 5, with a retinue of 40 men, Hamet at last made his appearance. The Kourchief released Mr. Eaton and the two midshipmen, and two days later, the rest of us laid eyes on the focus of our efforts. I dare say none of us were impressed.

Chapter 27

Marabout, Egypt
March 2, 1805

Jacob

"Sergeant Campbell, steady the men. No one will leave the Arab's Tower," Lieutenant O'Bannon ordered before striding off to meet the commander of the Turkish troops.

A week before, on February 23, Mr. Eaton, or I should say General Eaton now, signed a "Convention between the United States of America and his Highness, Hamet Qaramanli, Bashaw of Tripoli." This document had 14 articles, but the crux was that we would help the bashaw, as we were now told by that title to address him, regain the throne from his brother. In return, the bashaw would free the *Philadelphia* prisoners without ransom, repay the United States for the monetary support it was giving him for this endeavor, and grant the United States most-favored nation status. It also granted General Eaton the title of general and commander-in-chief of the invasion force.

The next week was spent gathering forces to march on Tripoli. This included hiring Greeks and Mamelukes as well as purchasing provisions and weapons.

While dockworkers of the bashaw were loading some supplies on a lateen-sailed *djerm* this morning, Turkish troops seized the vessel and arrested General Eaton. They began to march to us here in Marabout. Fearful that the bashaw would flee, General Eaton sent a messenger to Lieutenant O'Bannon with orders to keep the bashaw and his retinue in place in the Arab's Tower.

"Look lively, ladies. You heard the lieutenant," Sergeant Campbell said, as the seven of us turned not towards the advancing Turks but to our erstwhile allies.

We could see the bashaw's paladin being prepared, and more than a few of his servants made fits and starts as if to leave. Six Marine privates, though, in full uniform and standing shoulder to shoulder, muskets at the ready, created an imposing sight, I have to surmise, as not one person attempted to pass us.

"There are 50 of them," David Thomas whispered to me as he stood to my right. "Why don't they just rush us?"

"Quiet in the ranks," Sergeant Campbell ordered, his voice calm and assured.

David was correct in saying that if the mob wanted to flee, they could. But who wanted to be the one to wind up on a Marine bayonet or to eat a .69 caliber ball? I wanted to see if the lieutenant had reached the Turkish forces yet, but I had to stare at the bashaw's people with a most fierce countenance. I must confess that at first my heart was pounding in my breast, but as no one showed the least fortitude to try and push past us, I began to relax and, dare I say it, become bored? Although it was only March, the hot Egyptian sun pounded down on us, and sweat coursed down my back. I had a most annoying itch on my nose, but I forbore to scratch at it.

Before too long, Lieutenant O'Bannon came back and ordered us to stand down. The crisis had been averted. He went into the bashaw's quarters to sooth the timid man who had been most ready to abandon his quest to take the throne.

Later, we found out that the show of force was just that. A Turkish supervisor of revenue had been left out of the hands being fed good American dollars, and he wanted his share before he would allow us to depart. Mr. Biggs, the British consul, took care of this omission, and the Turkish troops, who Lieutenant O'Bannon had delayed outside of Marabout, were recalled.

Chapter 28

Marabout, Egypt
March 6, 1805

Jacob

"Where d'ya think Mr. Eaton got that uniform?" John Whitten asked, looking at the general as he tried to get all the elements of our motley force moving.

"That's General Eaton, John," I replied.

"But he's not a real general, is he?"

"I don't know if he is or not, but if it's good enough for Lieutenant O'Bannon, it's good enough for me. As for the uniform, he was a captain in the Legion of America, so I would think this is his old uniform, and he has added a few embellishments to it."

"I don't know much about that, but it don't seem right to me, him being a Navy Lieutenant one day and a general the next. And what about him saying he's the only son of 'Emperor Jefferson?'" he countered.

I merely shrugged. I had been taken aback by General Eaton's claim to kinship with the "emperor" as well, but if it helped on our mission, perhaps it was a lie well told. I knew he had fronted his own money for many of our expenses, and his drive to succeed was certainly laudable.

General Eaton, Lieutenant O'Bannon, and Mr. Peck, one of the Argus' midshipmen, were the only three Americans in a dress uniform. The seven enlisted Marines had carefully packed our new uniforms and were now in our new linen utilities. This was a Godsend, to be sure. The lieutenant wanted our uniforms to be in good condition when we met up with Yusef Bashaw's forces, so he ordered the utilities for the march through the desert. The utilities were a simple but sturdy pair of pants and a short jacket. These protected our bodies from the African sun, but were light enough so that even the slightest breeze could cool us. From a distance, though, with our hats and breastbands, I thought we would still look like a proper military force.

As far as the rest of our army, our appearances would not strike fear into any foes, I would guess. General Eaton, Lieutenant O'Bannon, Mr. Peck, Jean Eugene, and Mr. Farquhar had scoured Alexandria for troops to join us, and a more diverse army I've never seen.

Two Greek troops had joined us. Captain Ulovix commanded 25 artillerymen and one small field piece. Lieutenant Constantine commanded 38 infantrymen. On horseback were about 60 Bedouins in flowing white robes and blue veils commanded by Sheik Mohammed el Tayeb. Milling around were perhaps 400 infantry from various nationalities: Arabs, Turks, Levantines, Egyptians, all under the command of Selim Comb. Behind our army, another army of wives and unmarried women, cooks, children, drivers, over a hundred camels, and I don't know who else gathered, ready to follow us as we marched.

In the general's staff rode Mr. Farquhar, Jean Eugene, our Hungarian surgeon general, Dr. Mandreci, Lieutenant Rocco, an Italian, and the general's chief of staff, the Chevalier de Aries. In the center of all of this was Hamet Bashaw with his 90-person retinue. The bashaw was to be carried by a silk paladin.

With this force and the General leading the Marines right behind him, we marched off into the desert.

Chapter 29

30 Miles West of Marabout
March 8, 1805

Jacob

The Arabs went on strike, demanding that General Eaton pay them their total due at once instead of at our destination. It seemed that Sheik el Tayeb had told them that "the Christians" would not pay them once we arrived.

General Eaton refused their demand, and the Arabs sat down on the ground, saying they would not move another foot. The general tried to get the bahsaw to intervene, but that worthy would not express an opinion.

"Very well," the general said before turning to his chief-of-staff. "Mr. de Aries, please form up the men to return to Alexandria."

With that, he mounted his horse and turned around to retrace our route back. All of the Christian forces formed up and began to march. We whispered amongst ourselves as to what would happen to our mission. Was it over?

We had marched nary a mile before a mounted Arab galloped to meet us. He asked the general to return, telling him that the Arab forces would wait until the mission was completed before getting paid.

I caught a wry smile on the general's face when he ordered us to turn around yet one more time to continue our march toward Derne. With this display, I began to see why Lieutenant O'Bannon thought so highly of the man.

Jonathan P. Brazee

Chapter 30

The Qattara Depression
March 11, 1805

Jacob

The land we crossed was a series of rocky gullies, sandy outcroppings and dried washes. We rarely could see the entirety of the column. About mid-afternoon, a messenger rode up and told us that the people of Derne had revolted and were only awaiting the bashaw for deliverance. The governor had locked himself in the palace and had no support.

This later proved to be fantasy. There was no revolt in Derne. But upon hearing this, the bashaw's retinue was jubilant, as could be expected. When the word reached the Arab cavalry, they started riding around in a circle, firing their weapons into the air.

At the rear of the column, the Arab infantry heard the firing and assumed we were under attack by desert nomads. Not willing to give up the baggage train, they turned on the Greek infantry to kill them and take the baggage for themselves. Thirty-eight Greeks faced off against several hundred assorted Mahomaten troops.

Just as the two forces started to clash, an Arab officer interposed himself, ordering all to stand down until they could ascertain just what was happening. His quick thinking and forceful action prevented a massacre and saved the mission.

In the front of the column with the general, we never found out about the near-disaster until we made camp that evening. It was a sobering lesson for all. Our Arab allies might not be so staunch as we would have expected.

Chapter 31

Qattara Depression
March 13, 1805

Jacob

"Damn them all to hell!" Sergeant Campbell shouted, cutlass in hand as he strode back and forth, kicking up the sand.

He seemed ready to march to the Arab camp and demand satisfaction. We all felt the same, but seven Marines against a few hundred Arabs did not seem like a fair fight.

Theft had become a way of life on the march. Barley, rice, and provisions disappeared daily. They had even taken the polish for Mr. Peck's brass buttons, to his dismay. But this was going too far.

After we had put up our tent for the evening, we stacked our muskets in the usual fashion at the entrance. When we awoke the next morning, our muskets, along with our bayonets, ammunition, and cheese were gone.

A Marine is nothing without his musket, and all of us felt emasculated. I didn't envy Sergeant Campbell going to the lieutenant to tell him what happened. How could we let anyone steal our muskets?

We broke down our tent while we waited for our sergeant to return. When he did, he was accompanied by Lieutenant O'Bannon, who looked at where we had stacked arms, then looked at us.

"So none of you heard anything strange, such as the clatter of muskets being removed, while you slept? Not one of you?" he asked in an accusing tone.

There was nothing we could say, no excuse that was satisfactory.

He shook his head, then sighed. "Come with me. We will issue each of you a new musket. Make sure they are ready for use. I will decide how to handle this later."

After this incident, our muskets never left our possession. No more stacked arms either. We slept on them. They were not as soft a bed companion as our wives and ladies, but we kept them closer than any of us had kept a woman.

Chapter 32

Marsa Matrub
March 19, 1805

Jacob

Mr. Peck took a swallow of water and almost hashed it back out. As a young midshipman, he lacked in experience for all he made up in an officer's haughty manner. That lack of experience had cost him dearly.

With water sources few and far between, he had finally bartered for an Arab water skin. These skins were made with camel fat, greasing them inside and out to keep them from cracking in the hot sun. This made the taste of any water held therein extraordinarily vile. For the last several days, Mr. Peck had been reduced to drinking from this skin.

Mr. Peck had not endeared himself to us, yet I felt pity on him. I stood up and walked over to him, taking a bottle out of my haversack. I had rescued the bottle from the sand after the officers had toasted the start of the expedition with brandy. A good Marine never lets anything go to waste, so I had kept it, not knowing when I might make use of it. But Mr. Peck seemed to need it more.

"Here you are, sir. Perhaps this might make the water taste better," I said as I handed it to him.

I can't say if he looked at me with suspicion or not, but it might have been. Many officers did not trust an enlisted man for any motivation other than greed or slovenliness. He took the bottle, though.

"Thank you, Private Brissey," he said, beginning to pour the water from his skin into the bottle.

I held out my hand and stopped him.

"Begging your pardon, sir, but you might want to wait until you have clean water before putting any in there. If you pour that water, the camel fat will contaminate the bottle as well."

Many officers would take affront at being told what to do by a mere private, and I stood by to weather an assault. If he had the gumption to berate Mr. Farquhar, who was purportedly a lieutenant, what might he do with a private?

Instead of the thunder I expected, he stopped, looked at me, and smiled.

"I believe you are correct, Private Brissey. Again, I must offer you my thanks."

He slipped the bottle into his haversack and offered his hand, much to my surprise. We shook like two men, equal in terms. Not knowing what else to do after he released his grip, I saluted, then went back to the rest of the Marines.

"How did it taste?" Bernard O'Brien asked as I came up.

I looked at him without comprehension. Was he referring to the water?

"I mean, with your gan[25] so far up Mr. Peck's feak. How was it?"

The rest of the squad laughed, and I felt my face go red.

"Not that you would know compassion, you pumpkin.[26] We all know how tight paddies are with a penny," I retorted, eliciting more laughter.

"Aye, we know the value of a dollar, not like you Southerners."

I had to laugh at that. Only someone from Boston could call a New Yorker a "Southerner." Except for the lieutenant, though, I was the southern-most native amongst the Marines. The rest had all been recruited in Massachusetts, Connecticut, and Maine.

I looked around at the others. We six had been chosen for this mission, and I dared to think that was because of the perception of our worth. Most of the Marines were still aboard the *Argus*, and some of them, well, suffice it to say that I was most pleased that it was these five with whom I was now marching to Derne.

Bernard O'Brien was a cock-sure young fellow, bold but with the physicality to back himself up. He had the red hair of an Irishman, but despite my calling him a "paddy," he had no trace of the Irish brogue. He

---

[25] Gan: mouth or lips, especially in a sexual connotation
[26] Pompkin: a Bostonian (because of their partiality to eating pumpkins)

cut a mean jig, though, especially when the lieutenant was playing his fiddle. The scuttlebutt was that he might soon make corporal.

James Owens was a fisherman's son from Maine, from the same town as our illustrious general. He was a quiet sort, bookish. We shared some interesting discussions on books we had read, and I was sometimes surprised at his insight. He never complained, and he was the only non-drinker in our group. To save money, I didn't drink much, but James drank nary a drop.

On the other hand, Edward Steward made up for him on that. Edward loved life, and he spent every penny enjoying it to the fullest. In Cairo and Alexandria, he was the first to find the nanny houses, and he made more use of them than anyone else, Marine or sailor. He was a small man, but he had extraordinary stamina, both on the march, and if the others could be believed, in bed.

David Thomas was a Connecticut lad, one who tended to question things. He wondered whether the bashaw even deserved to be put on the throne. I daresay that all of us had thought as much, given the less-than-admirable man himself, but only Dave put voice to those doubts. Not as stout as the rest of us, he suffered a bit more during the march.

The last of us was John Whitten. He was the one who kept our spirits up, whether singing or telling tales as long and as convoluted as can be imagined. Already, he had kept us entertained while we marched, telling tales of derring-do and far off lands. His pate[27] was already bare, and with his fair skin, the sun turned him as red as the lobsters the poor of his native Cape Cod were forced to eat.

Lieutenant O'Bannon told us that we should be getting another 100 Marines when we got resupplied in Bomba, but for now, I was pleased with my companions. It would have been good to have Seth and Ichabod with us, but we made for a good squad.

"Mount up, ladies," Sergeant Campbell ordered as he rushed up, breathing hard. "The general needs us now."

We jumped up, grabbed our muskets, then went with him to where the general, Lieutenant O'Bannon, Mr. de Vries, and Mr. Peck were arguing with the head camel drover, a man we called "Big Belly." We formed on either side of him, but the drover was not backing down.

---

[27] Pate: head

113

Through the interpreter, he was insisting that he had been hired only to Marsa Matrub, and that was as far as the $11 paid per camel was going to get them. The general vacillated between arguing and pleading, but Big Belly would not move an iota. Finally, the general ordered us to remain in position while he strode off to see the bashaw, who was lounging in his pavilion.

Big Belly smirked at us while we waited in the afternoon sun. I felt that he was attempting the old trick of bargaining for one thing, then trying to renegotiate for more when he had us over the barrel. We had to have camels in order to march.

When the general came back, I thought he would give Big Belly the what for, but instead, he ordered us back about 10 yards. His face was red with anger, but he controlled his fury. He told us the bashaw had indeed only negotiated for the camels to go to Marsa Matrub, keeping the rest of the money advanced to him for himself. Now, with only $540 left of the money Lieutenant Hull had given, he needed to raise enough to pay Big Belly.

With what looked to be sincere embarrassment, he asked all of us to give what we could. I only had $11 in my pocket, what with half of my salary being in an allotment to Suva. Edward, not surprisingly, had spent every penny in Cairo and Alexandria. But between the officers and the rest of the Marines, we gave the general $140. With this, he hurried off to Big Belly, who had left us to start preparing his caravan for the march back to Egypt.

After receiving the money, Big Belly announced that they would continue the journey. We made camp under the old ruined castle that was Marsa Matrub, grateful that we still had our camels. That gratitude was short-lived as when we awoke the next morning, we found out that a full 70 camel drivers had slipped out during the night, with American dollars in hand.

The remaining 40 drivers seemed upset that they had been left behind, and while the general tried to rectify the situation, they too deserted us. The general was livid, exclaiming that these same men would accept huge hardships to make their pilgrimage to Mecca, but here they deserted at the slightest provocation.

"Cash is the only deity of the Arabs," he lamented once he was told that the remaining camels were gone.

At this critical time, the Arabs had a council, and at midnight, asked the general to attend. Bernard and I accompanied him into the tent where Sheik el Tayeb approached us and told the general that his men would not march any farther unless a messenger was sent to Bomba to see whether the *Argus* and the *Nautilus* had arrived with fresh provisions and funds. The reality was that the Arabs had heard rumors that Yusef Bashaw had sent a force of 800 infantry and cavalry to reinforce Derne, and that force had already reached Benghazi.

By this time, we were down to only rice and biscuits, and precious little of that. It would take a messenger ten days to go to Bomba and back while we consumed our dwindling rations. General Eaton looked at the sheik for a long moment, then calmly announced that rations would henceforth be given only to those who were continuing. He turned and walked out, followed by the two of us.

"Mr. O'Bannon, kindly form your Marines and the Greeks around the rations. Not one Arab will receive any of them until further notice."

"Aye-aye, general."

He turned to Sergeant Campbell and Captain Ulovix and gave his orders. The lone field piece would be placed in the center of the formation, the Marines flanking it, bayonets fixed. Behind us would be the Greeks. Once we formed, I daresay we made for an impressive show of fortitude.

Several of the Arab greybeards came over to look at us, muttering amongst themselves. Sheik el Tayeb seemed to be in the middle of it all, and even though I could not speak Arabic, I could tell that not everyone was in agreement. They left and disappeared back towards their camp. About an hour later, the sheik came back and asked to speak with the general. Sergeant Campbell sent Dave back to fetch him.

When the general returned, the Sheik took his hand and warmly shook it, explaining that they were all friends, that of course his men would be happy to continue on. He told us he had sent men to retrieve the last 40 camels that had left, and that they had never "refused" to march; they had only wanted to express some concerns.

It looked like our trek could continue.

Chapter 33

The Camp of the Eu ed Alli
Cyrenaica Plateau, Libya
March 23, 1805

Jacob

"Well, lookie at that," Edward exclaimed, stopping dead in his tracks.

My head had been down as I climbed the ridge, so I bumped into him before I could stop. I looked up to see what he meant. After miles upon parched miles in the dry and rocky desert, the green plain in front of me was a jolt of color. On the plain, the Eu ed Alli Bedouins gathered with their thousands of camels and sheep. Mr. Peck had told me that there were 4,000 in the tribe, and that they were all staunch allies of the bashaw. The smell of cooking fires wafted over to us.

"You think we'll get some food? I mean real food?" Bernard asked.

As the largest Marine, if not the largest man in the entire march, he struggled on the meager rations to which we had been reduced. But he was not alone in that. My own mouth watered at the thought of a hearty repast.

"Let's look sharp, ladies," Sergeant Campbell ordered, walking down our line.

Coming up the ridge, we had straggled into a longer line, but at the sergeant's urging, we formed up into two columns. I could feel the strength flow into my limbs. We were relying on the Bedouin's succor, so we had to look like we deserved it.

The officers had a hard time calming their mounts, which started prancing at the smell of fresh grass ahead. I didn't think that was too bad a thing. It made all of us look more ready for a fight should it come to that.

As the bashaw's entourage crested the ridge in back of us, we could hear the shouts of joy. I looked back as they reveled in the moment. Only the slaves holding the bashaw's paladin didn't change their expression. I thought they would be the most overjoyed, ready to put their heavy burden down. But they merely looked resigned to the long descent into the plains.

As we reached the grasslands, the smells hit me first. After only dust, the fresh grassy scent and the smell of livestock were a welcome respite. We marched behind the mounted officers as we entered the encampment. The Bedouins, in their white *barracans*, clustered around us, gawking at our weapons and dress. The women did not wear veils. I sensed no hostility from them, only happy curiosity. When Sergeant Campbell ordered us to halt, he ordered a manual of arms to ground our muskets. The people broke out into excited comments while some of the tykes laughed in glee. For the first time since leaving the *Argus*, I truly felt welcomed.

While we waited for the officers to greet the local sheiks, a number of Bedouins came to us to barter. I had given my last $11 to the general, so I had no money. However, the Bedouins seemed more interested in brass buttons. John had at least 20 buttons in his haversack—to what end, I don't know to this day—but it was a happy circumstance as he traded one for a sack of fresh dates. He spread them around, and I am not sure when I have ever enjoyed such thick sweetness.

Edward kept asking John to loan him some buttons, his eyes on the friendly ladies amongst the men who crowded around us. John was saved though, by Sergeant Campbell's stern warning.

"There will be none of that, Private Steward. You'll have to keep your sugar stick[28] in your pants."

"But sergeant, look at them. They's ready for some American sausage, I thinks!"

"And all those men beside them? You think they'll just stand by while you clicket[29] their women-folk?" the sergeant went on.

"Well, I donst care if they join us, I donst. The more the merrier," Dave replied, looking wistfully around him.

We all broke into laughter. How much he was serious and how much was bravado, I wasn't sure. I wouldn't put much past him, though.

"Ah, I'd probably catch the blue boar[30], anyhew," he said as the sergeant turned back away. "Might be worth it, though."

---

[28] Sugar stick: penis
[29] Clicket: to have sex

Jonathan P. Brazee

I ate the last of my date, trying to ignore the men pushing gazelles and sheep at us. I had never tried gazelle and would like to, but I didn't think I had enough buttons to afford one.

Lieutenant O'Bannon came out of the main tent and walked toward us.

"Sergeant Campbell, set up camp over there," he said, pointing to the southern fringe of the vast encampment. "Make sure the general's tent is next to yours on the outside. We don't expect any trouble, but better safe than sorry."

"What time will we be marching out in the morning, sir?" Sergeant Campbell asked.

"We're not. Get ready for a few days of rest and relaxation. Some of these Bedouins will join us when we leave, but General Eaton thinks the bashaw needs a few days to rest first."

Three days of rest? With fresh food? It was a happy squad of Marines that rushed to comply with his orders.

---

[30] Blue Boar: a type of venereal disease

Chapter 34

The Camp of the Eu ed Alli
Cyrenaica Plateau, Libya
March 28, 1805

Jacob

Our three days of rest rejuvenated us. The Bedouins entertained us with horsemanship contests, and I dare say they could give the best American horsemen a run for their money. These were a happy, contented people, and 80 cavalry and 150 infantry agreed to join us on our march.

On the American side, the general demonstrated his skill with a rifle, to their great admiration. He even shot the head off a desert rat at 50 paces, something nigh impossible with one of our Charlevilles.

Lieutenant O'Bannon impressed them with his fiddle playing. His favorite music, "Hogs in the Corn," had them stamping their feet and shouting with gusto. I am not sure what they thought of Bernard dancing a jig to the lieutenant's playing, but I enjoyed their attempts to ape Bernard and his movements.

The Bedouins were particularly taken with our buttons, which they imagined to be made of gold. We had changed from linens to our dress uniforms while at their encampment, and to them, it seemed that even the lowest of us were rich beyond means. They openly remarked that it was surprising that God would permit us to possess such riches being that we were followers of the religion of the devil. Here, the general's comments served to help sway them. As he had in Cairo, he insisted that the religion of the Americans was not different from theirs, and that we were all Abraham's children. He told them that of all the "nations who wore hats," only ours embraced people of all creeds.

Both Bernard as a fervent Papist and Jim as an equally devout Presbyterian took offense at that, and we all had to restrain Bernard from

Jonathan P. Brazee

confronting the general on the issue. We had to present a united front, and we were only privates after all, but both men felt that the Lord himself held sway over mere generals, and His honor had to be protected.

While the Bedouins had food aplenty, they became quite taken with our biscuits, much to our astonishment. They broke them up with their scimitars and clubs, then relished the crumbs. Rice was even a greater delicacy. One woman offered her daughter, a voluptuous hazel-eyed 14-year-old, to the general's interpreter for a sack of rice. The daughter was in agreement to the arrangement, but the general forbade it on prudence grounds.

Alas, this welcomed respite was too good to be true, as these things most often are. On the 26th, a messenger arrived with word that Yusef Bashaw's forces were but a few days out of Derne. This caused a great deal of consternation, not only amongst the Arabs, but also within the bashaw's entourage. Several of the bashaw's advisors begged him to turn back to Cairo, and the general's nemesis, Sheik el Tayeb announced he would move no farther until there was proof that our ships awaited us at Bomba. General Eaton broke into a great rage, calling the sheik every pejorative in his vocabulary, and that was a very impressive list. The sheik stormed off, swearing by all the force of the prophet that he would join us no more. The general ordered the rations withheld again, so the Greeks and we Marines were back to guard duty over our supplies.

The bashaw begged the general to send a messenger to the sheik to try and convince him to return, but the general refused. Instead, the general sent a messenger to tell the sheik that if he had become our enemy, the general had the right to seek him out and punish him.

In the morning, we formed up and started our march, less the sheik and those Bedouins whom the sheik had convince to abandon our cause. We heard that the sheik had started his march to return to Egypt, so the general sent him a message that upon completion of our mission, he would seek out the sheik to recover the cash and property he had "so fraudulently received."

Two hours later, another messenger reached us, this time asking us to stop so the sheik's forces could rejoin us. When the sheik made his appearance, he strode up to the general with a huge smile on his face, proudly noting the influence he had with his people, as if he had never been part of the problem but was rather the solution.

120

We stopped for the night, but in the morning, the bashaw took back some of the horses so his own staff could ride. Lieutenant O'Bannon and Mr. Peck were now afoot.

The general had learned some lessons, though. He ordered us to fix bayonets, but instead of the staff leading the march, he put the camels in the lead with the Marines in trace. He was determined that no more camels would disappear from our army.

Camels are not the serene creatures depicted in books. In reality, they are vile, dirty, and obnoxious animals, the very devil's mounts. We had been trained to fight in the tops; we had been trained in ground combat. I never dreamed that I would be serving as a shepherd to these horrible creatures. I made a solemn oath on the Libyan plateau that once this mission was accomplished, I would never go near a camel again.

Chapter 35

Cyrenaica Plateau, Libya
March 29, 1805

Jacob

I was roused from my sleep when Dave shook my foot. My eyes were gritty as I opened them. After a day following the camels, I was filthy, but I knew I had to get up at midnight to stand sentry, so excepting my belt and shoes, I had decided to sleep in the rough. I just didn't have the energy to remove my shirt, pantaloons, and linens.

"Wake up, Jacob, the general wants to see you," he told me.

My heart raced as I wondered what I had done to catch his notice. I wished I had taken the time to wash up before falling asleep, but there was nothing to be done about that now. I grabbed one shoe, pulling it on and lacing it up. The other shoe followed, but when I put in my foot, I felt a small hard object in there, one that moved.

"Holy Trinity!" I shouted, flinging the shoe to the ground.

One of the curses of Africa was the scorpion, the deadly little beast with the huge stinger. They had a habit of creeping into boots during the night, ready to sting unwary feet. We all had seen it when one of the Moors had been stung, and his cries of agony were not something any of us wanted to be forced to make ourselves. We all made it part of our routine to shake out our boots before putting them on, but in my haste to report to the general, I had forgotten to do so. I checked my foot carefully, fearful that I had been stung.

"What ails you, Jacob?" John asked.

"Scorpion! In my shoe," I shouted back, heart pounding in my breast.

"In the truth?" he asked. "Let me see."

With that, he reached in my shoe with his bare hand, much to my horror. I reached out to stop him, only he screamed in agony before I could do anything. He fell to the ground, writhing in pain. I reached him, pulling on his arm to see his clenched fist. I hesitated, fearing what I would see, but I grasped his fingers and forced open his hand. There in his palm, was a large black beetle, one of the thousands we had seen in the desert swarming over the dung left by the camels. I could not fathom what had happened until the rest of the squad erupted into laughter.

"Here's your scorpion," John told me, dropping the beetle into my lap as he broke into peals of laughter.

I felt relief flow over me, but relief coated with anger. I knew John had planned the entire episode, chortling for hours as he put his mission into action. I picked up the beetle and threw it with all my might at John, hitting him right in his left eye.

"Ah! You got my eye," he shouted as he fell back, trying to laugh and shout at the same time.

"Serves you right, you, you tarnal[31] bastard!"

The laughing stopped for a moment before starting again, even louder than before.

"Reverend Brissey! You do know how to curse!" Bernard exclaimed, himself laughing uproariously.

Even I had to start laughing. It was a good prank, even if I was the object of it. I was a bit embarrassed to fall into coarse language, but I was with Marines, not genteel ladyfolk. I sat back down, reaching to take my left boot back off.

"Jacob, the general really does wants to see you," Dave told me. "John took advantage of it, but it's the truth."

I looked at him closely to see if this was part of the joke.

"Brissey, where are you?" Sergeant Campbell's voice reached us from outside the tent. "You better be coming out in 10 seconds or there'll be a reckoning!"

There was more laughing, but with the help of the others, I got on my right boot and belt, grabbed my musket and hat, and rushed out of the tent. Sergeant Campbell merely glared at me, a scowl on his face, then he strode off with me in trace. He reached the general's tent before I did,

---

[31] Tarnal: a general curse word

stuck his head inside and said something, then stepped back, holding the flap open for me to enter. I didn't hesitate and stepped inside, marching to the general to stand before him at attention.

"Private Brissey, sir!" I announced myself.

"Ah, yes, Private Brissey. Mr. O'Bannon here tells me you have a fine hand. I want you to do your best to write what I have to tell you. It is vital that this document stand the test of time."

He indicated a small desk and chair with paper and a quill ready for me. I nodded and sat down as he got back into discussions with the lieutenant, Mr. Peck, and Mr. Farquhar. After about 20 minutes, he nodded at me to begin.

Over the next few hours, with starts and stops as they discussed wording, I penned a long message to the citizens of Tripoli, expressing our love for them and the closeness of our peoples and religions, of how the Christian God and the Mahomaten God were one and the same. The message told them of the deeds of Yusef and how Sid Hamet Bashaw was there to lead them into peace and prosperity.

The final few sentences of the letter struck me deeply:

We shall furnish you with war supplies and with food supplies, with money and, in case of your need, with regular soldiers to aid you in vanquishing ... your oppressor. And I shall be always with you until the end of the war and even until you have achieved your glorious mission, in proof of our fidelity and goodwill.

The United States was dedicated to freedom for all men, and I believed this letter was proof of that. Not only was freedom desirable for us, but for all men who slaved under tyranny. This was something in which I could believe, something I could support with all my being.

Chapter 36

Tripoli
March 30, 1805

Ichabod

Life in Tripoli had gotten a mite better seeing as how our bombardment had ended. Some of our drivers even began to show a human face. Suddenly, though, we were rushed back to our jail, and our drivers looked most concerned.

We didn't know the reason until Mr. Cowdery made his appearance. The bashaw had received intelligence that the Americans were marching on Tripoli to place his older brother on the throne. He had first asked Mr. Cowdery how many Marines the Americans had. Mr. Cowdery told him there were 10,000 Marines in the force.

"He was most concerned about our Marines, but when I told him we had 80,000 others under arms and a million militia, he became most somber. He is most concerned now, as he cannot raise any more levies."

We laughed at his cleverness, but then he became more serious.

"I am here to convey some grievous news, however. Captain Bainbridge does not lend much credence to Mr. Eaton's efforts, but the bashaw is convinced that Eaton's force will reach Tripoli this summer. As such, he has vowed to execute all of us rather than let us be freed."

We all fell silent, suddenly sober as a judge. Our eventual freedom was the only thing that kept us going. The thought that our suffering would only end in our death was almost more than we could bear.

"Don't give up hope, lads. Captain Bainbridge is sure Eaton's force will never make it across the desert."

I donst know which thought was worse, that our rescue might never arrive, or that our rescue would result in our death.

Jonathan P. Brazee

Chapter 37

Cyrenaica Plateau, Libya
April 1, 1805

Jacob

"Donst it ever stop raining here?" Dave asked as we huddled inside our tent, the rain drops a staccato drum roll as it hit the canvas.

"First it's the heat, now the rain. What would it take to make you happy there, Marine?" John said with a laugh.

John had it right. Dave complained about nigh on everything: the heat, the cold, the food (or lack thereof), the bashaw, the Arabs, the rocky path we trod.

"Hot or cold, this is surely Satan's land, and I daresay we should leave it to the Arab, Mameluke, Turk, or whoever wants it."

Waiting in the cold rain for the bashaw to return had been less than agreeable. We had asked if we could put on our dress uniforms, knowing we would be warmer, but Sergeant Campbell refused, telling us we had to keep them in good condition.

Just then, the entrance to our tent opened as Bernard made his entrance, letting the rain blow in as we shouted out our displeasure. Edward hastily closed the ties to keep as much of the wet out as possible.

"Or you can be like our ankle[32] there, Private O'Brien, with a child in the belly to keep you warm," John went on.

Without warmer wear, Bernard had taken his blanket and stuffed it inside his shirt, and as John had alluded, it did make him look as if he was with child. Bernard cupped his hands in front of his belly, as if protecting his gravid condition. He purposely stumbled, then stepped on John's outstretched foot.

---

[32] Ankle: a pregnant woman

"Oh, excuse me, good sir," he said in a high falsetto, "I can't seem to keep my stead, what with my condition. But you can blame this Marine," he went on, pointing at Edward. "He has taken my virtue, the niffynaffy[33] fellow!"

John pushed Bernard down, then jumped on him.

"You slattern! You told me the child was my by blow!" he shouted, then bounced up and down on the laughing Bernard, who kept protesting his innocence in his high falsetto.

"Hey, watch it," shouted James as the rest of us laughed as well. "You'll bring down the tent, and I have no desire to get even more wet."

That brought out even more laughter, although why that struck us as funny, I have nary a clue. We did begin to settle down though, to wait for the bashaw to return with the missing Arabs.

"D'ya know what I miss most?" Edward asked to no one in particular.

"Yes, you mutton monger[34], we know what you miss," John retorted.

"No, I mean, yeah, I miss that. But what I really miss right now is bacon, hot sizzling bacon."

We all groaned. The mere thought of bacon made the soggy handful of rice we were rationed each day seem even more vile. My stomached growled at the thought.

"Oh, good Lord, bacon. I like mine crispy, I do," I said, unable to help myself.

"No, Jacob, you needs it all soft and greasy, sos the fat drips out your muns," Dave added.

Our conversation drifted for the next half hour, with thoughts of bacon, roast beef, apples, tripe, clams, white bread and butter, and all other delicious and most missed foods. We knew we would be happier without those thoughts in our heads, but like a scab that had to be picked, we couldn't resist.

Sergeant Campbell interrupted our reverie when he opened our tent flap and called out, "Up'n at 'em, ladies. The general's at it again, and the lieutenant wants us aside him."

---

[33] Niffynaffy: a trifler
[34] Mutton monger: a lecher

We all jumped up and scrambled for our hats, ammo pouches, and belts. We had become experts at dressing within the small confines of our tent, and within moments we were outside in full kit. We formed up and marched to the general's tent where he was in great form as he exploded at Sheik el Tayeb. Evidently, the sheik had asked that the rice rations be increased, and the general was in a tirade.

He blamed the sheik for our delays, telling him that he had promised we would be in Derne in fourteen days, and here some 26 days later, we were not even half-way there.

The sheik responded that he was a better man than the general, and that without an increased rice ration and biscuits, there would be an insurrection. To this, the general told him that if there was an insurrection, he would personally hunt the sheik down and put him to death.

With that, the sheik whirled away and mounted his horse. It wasn't until some five hours later that the sheik went to Mr. Peck and Mr. Farquhar's tent and asked them to tell the general that he was a loyal man, and that the coming battle at Derne would prove that.

"That's iffen we ever make Derne," Dave said when we heard that. "With all the fighting with our own Arabs, iffen we ever make Derne, it'll be a relief to meet enemies who stand afore us as enemies, not like friends who'd just as soon stab you as not."

For once, none of us took issue with Dave's pessimism.

Chapter 38

Cyrenaica Plateau, Libya
April 3, 1805

Jacob

The gunfire took us by surprise.

"Form up, form up!" Sergeant Campbell shouted.

It took a moment to register, but we formed two ranks and rushed back towards the Bedouin camp at the double time, muskets at the ready. The general galloped past us, and we knew we had to hurry so as he would not face whatever danger reared its ugly head alone. Lieutenant O'Bannon caught up with us and joined our advance, cutlass in one hand, pistol in the other.

We crested the small ridge that separated our area of the encampment from the Bedouins. We expected almost anything—but not what we saw. General Eaton had reined in his horse, and just beyond him, a more fantastic sight I have rarely seen.

Two camels were festooned with braids, silks, and gold and silver chains. Horsemen were riding back and forth on either side of the camels, performing what displays of riding skills they possessed. Riding the camels was the focus of the celebration, for a celebration it was. On one camel, covered with brightly colored silk, was a bride, and on the other, the groom. The Bedouins were celebrating a wedding. Their gunfire had been part of their joy on the happy occasion.

The wedding party bade us to join them. Sergeant Campbell looked at the lieutenant, who gave his approval, so we joined several of the officers who were also drawn to the shooting.

We began a circuit of the Bedouin encampment, often stopping so the men could dance. Their lascivious moves would have made a lady of easy virtue blush, so graphic were they. But all took them in good stead,

Jonathan P. Brazee

laughing and shouting back to the groom. I may not have understood their words, but there was no misunderstanding their meaning.

The procession made its way to the Christian encampment, encircling it, then to the Arab encampment. More people joined in the procession, and men of different nations offered dances of their own style each time we stopped.

Finally, we returned to the Bedouin encampment once more. The camel with the bride was led around a tent seven times, then the camel was made to kneel, propelling the woman headfirst into the tent. General Eaton gave two dollars each to the parents of the bride.

We expected the groom to enter the tent next, but he got off his camel and left in the company of the other men. We were told that the young lady—at 13 years old, she was barely more than a girl—had to remain in the tent for three days before the marriage could be consummated. A matron would stay in the tent with her to assure that she was, in fact, kept isolated.

"Aye, tough luck on that," Edward said when we heard the news. "All that dancing and suggestion can get a man randy right quick, and now he has to wait for nigh on three days."

"No worry, sir," Tahnoon, one of the interpreters, told him. "The groom, he is a sheik and has three other wives. That woman there," he said, pointing at a woman I had assumed to be the bride's mother, "she is the senior wife. The sheik, he has seen over 50 years, so he can surely wait three more nights to sample his new wife."

"Over 50 years old? And now four wives, one of them 13 years old? I must doff my hat to the man. Back in Boston, we'd call him a buck fitch[35], a man with a colt's tooth[36] in his head, what with him taking such a young wife. But here, you call him a sheik. Mayhaps we can learn a bit from you folks."

"Only in your dreams, Edward, only in your dreams," John told him with a laugh.

"Aye, but what dreams they are!"

We straggled back to our tent. We would be taking over sentry duty to guard our stores from the Greeks in a few hours, and every Marine knew

---

[35] Buck fitch: an old lecher
[36] Colt's tooth: an older man with a younger mistress or wife

130

to relax whenever the opportunity presented itself. The excitement and festivity of the marriage was catching, though. My heart was still racing, my mien most uplifted. My own marriage to Suva had been a more somber, Christian affair, but while Edward's comments were in jest, there was a kernel of truth to them. I was a long way from New York, farther than I ever dreamed I would be. Much of what I had witnessed in Egypt and Libya was perplexing and much was annoying. But some was fascinating, and I couldn't help but wonder if some of their manners and customs could find a welcome hearth back in the United States.

Chapter 39

Suani Samaluth, Libya
April 5, 1805

Jacob

Thirst became the overriding concern of the force, which now numbered about 1,200 in fighters and camp followers. We did not have the means to carry much water other than our canteens and skins, expecting to replenish our supplies at each cistern and well. Last night, though, the cistern was dry and the well offered only sulphurous, salty, vile water. Around the well were numerous graves of *hajis*, likely who had died of thirst.

We marched through the night to find water, and nine of the bashaw's horses were stolen in the dark. By daylight, another horse had died from thirst and exhaustion. Finally, at about noon, we came upon the next well. It had water, thank the Lord, even if it was fetid and salty.

The entire army and followers crowded the well, anxious to drink even this vile liquid. Water, any water, was life, and we had to drink. Our food was down to a handful of rice, and hunger was our constant companion, but water was what occupied our minds.

We were tired, exhausted, and weak. Even Dave stopped his incessant complaining. It took too much energy to do so, I expect.

Without a good source of water, our mission was doomed, and our very lives were in jeopardy.

Chapter 40

The Libyan Desert
April 8, 1805

Jacob

The water was the most delicious elixir I had ever tasted in my short life. We drank until our bellies bloated, then used more to wash the Libyan sand from our necks and faces.

"I never thought I'd say water was better than ale, but I thinks iffen I is given a choice, I will takes this every time," Dave said, echoing what we all thought.

It had still been morning when we marched down the switchback, coming around a corner to see this reservoir of cool, clean water that had pooled at the bottom of the canyon. The animals, even the camels, rushed into it, their normal grunts and groans lost as they drank. For once, our column hurried to catch up as word of the water reached them.

The general had only taken a quick drink before riding off with Selim and Mr. Farquhar to scout the region, so we stood by, guarding the rice. Now that we had water, our thoughts turned to our dwindling supply of food.

"Look at that," James said, pointing to where the bashaw's entourage looked to be setting up camp. "Did the general order us to make camp here?"

The lieutenant looked up at that, a frown on his face. He stood up and walked over to see what was going on.

"You think we'll camp here?" Dave asked.

"I doubt it. We may have water, but we've only six days of rice left. We need to reach Bomba and get resupplied," I responded.

About 15 minutes later, the general returned, and seeing the bahsaw's camp being made, strode over. Sergeant Campbell caught our eyes, then simply tilted his head in the general's direction, so the six of us got up and followed him to be within easy reach should the general need us.

The bashaw was telling the general that he needed rest, and he wanted to remain where there was water until he could be assured that there were supplies waiting for us at Bomba.

"We may have water, but we won't have food if we tarry," the general told him. "We must move on."

The bashaw blamed the sheiks and tribal leaders, telling the general that they wanted a chance to rest.

"If they prefer famine to fatigue, they might have their choice!" was General Eaton's response.

"Mr. O'Bannon, cut off all rations to all of those who are not ready to march," he said before storming off.

Lieutenant O'Bannon looked up at the sacks of rice still on the camels. "Sergeant Campbell, erect the supply tent and put all the rice inside. Get the Greeks to assist and make sure no one has access to the stores."

We spent the next 30 minutes rushing to comply, then another five hours standing by, something at which we had gotten quite proficient during our march. Standing by seemed to be what we did most often.

Finally, the bashaw came out of his discussions with the sheiks and announced that all the Mahomatens would be returning to Egypt. They began breaking camp.

"Do you think we'll keep going?" Dave asked as we watched them break camp.

"Look at the general. Does he look like he's about to give up?" Bernard responded.

The general looked like nothing was amiss. He nonchalantly spoke with his staff, occasionally pointing forward, towards Bomba, as if discussing the next day's march.

Some of the Arabs and Bedouins were gathering in groups, and the general sent his interpreter to find out why. The man came back with the news that they intended to take the rice with them, leaving us with nothing.

The general spun around, shouting for the drummer. A moment later, we heard the beat to arms, but we were already moving back towards the tent, blocking the entrance. A few moments later, the Greeks rushed up and formed in back of us in a semicircle.

The Arabs gestured and conferred, but they seemed unwilling to confront us. They moved back, mounted their horses, and left, immediately followed by the bashaw and his men. They disappeared around a bend, leaving us alone.

"That's it then? It's just us?" Edward asked.

"Quiet back there," the general ordered.

Sergeant Campbell glared at Edward, who merely shrugged. We stood there in the sun, still blocking entry to the tent for about an hour before we heard approaching hoofbeats.

"Stand ready, ladies," Sergeant Campbell told us.

The Hamet Bashaw was the first one to make an appearance, followed by the rest of his staff and primary sheiks. He rode up to the general and told him that he had convinced the sheiks to stay with the army. He then ordered his servants to begin making camp.

The general visibly relaxed. It seemed as if the Arabs had backed down yet again to his will. He started to walk off before a thought seemed to strike him. To this day, I don't know if he wanted one more show of force or not, but he turned to Lieutenant O'Bannon and ordered a manual of arms.

Lieutenant O'Bannon saluted and echoed the order to Captain Ulovix. The lieutenant moved to our fore, then began the commands, but not before reminding us that this was a drill, that we would not actually fire.

At "load arms," the Arabs and Tripolitans stopped what they were doing around camp and looked at us with varying degrees of curiosity and concern. Through "open pans" and on up the chain of commands to "return ramrod," they became more agitated. But at "shoulder arms," "make ready," and "present," panic ensued.

The Arabs rushed to their mounts, shouting, "The Christians are preparing to fire at us!"

Meanwhile, we had been given the command "order arms," and were standing at attention, waiting for our next command. The bashaw himself had mounted and was ordering a charge. We waited in silence, not having received another order. I could sense more than see some of the

Greek infantry step away and back out of the formation, as did Mr. de Aries, the general's chief of staff.

Two hundred mounted Arab warriors wheeled their mounts and galloped into the charge.

"What do we do now?" Bernard whispered.

"Steady, lads," Sergeant Campbell whispered back, not moving a muscle.

The Arabs looked fierce as they thundered down on us. My attention was drawn to one of them, his face twisted in a grimace, his hate evident. I knew he wanted to see us dashed to pieces on the desert ground. Just as it looked like they would run over us, they slid to a halt, dust billowing out in front of them to descend upon us. There was much shouting, and they aimed their muskets at the general, the lieutenant, Mr. Peck, and Mr. Farquhar.

In Arabic, we heard someone shout out *"Atlq,"* or "Fire!"

Immediately, one of the bashaw's officers stepped forward shouting, *"W'allahi,* in the name of Allah, do not fire! The Christians are our friends!"

At this, the general turned to the lieutenant and handed him his saber, rifle, and pistols, then marched forward to meet the milling Arabs. He started haranguing the bashaw. At once, all the muskets were aimed directly at his chest.

One Arab rode a few steps closer, put a pistol at Mr. Farquhar's chest, and pulled the trigger. All we heard was a click. Whether the pistol misfired or had never been loaded, we never knew.

The general grabbed the now dismounted bashaw by the arm and started to lead him away. One of his retainers tried to stop him from going with the general, but the bashaw struck the man with the flat of his scimitar, almost causing an outbreak of fighting as some thought the bashaw was under attack.

The bashaw was able to stop his men, and after some conversation, he agreed with the general to stand down his cavalry. The two men went into General Eaton's tent, and when they emerged, the bashaw ordered his camp be set up once again. The emergency was over, for the moment at least.

During this entire time, we had been standing at attention, moving nary a muscle. It took some fortitude, I will admit, when the Arab horsemen were charging us, but we held our position.

General Eaton came up to us, pride evident on his face. He grabbed the lieutenant in a deep embrace, calling him "My brave American!"

After the general released his embrace, Lieutenant O'Bannon attempted to chastise him. "General Eaton, how could you go into their midst without a weapon? How can we protect you without being at your side?"

The general laughed, lifted up his arms, and by flexing his wrists, two of his throwing knives jumped from beneath his sleeves and into his hands, ready for action.

"I trust you and your Marines implicitly, but sometimes, a man's got to look out for himself."

He pushed the knives back down until they caught on whatever harness held them at the ready. He clapped the lieutenant on the shoulder, then turned and strode off.

After the general left, the lieutenant turned to look at us. "Gentlemen, I'm honored. Sergeant Campbell, dismiss the men."

Our sergeant saluted, then turned to face us. "You heard the lieutenant, men. Dismissed."

"What, no 'ladies,' sergeant? You going soft on us?" John asked, and suddenly the pent up tension fled our bodies.

"I reckon for today, at least, you shown yourself to be men."

James pounded my back as we walked back to where we had pitched our tent. "That was something," he said excitedly, showing more emotion perhaps than I had witnessed in him before.

"Weren't nothing," Edward casually remarked.

All of us to a man stopped to stare at him. Facing down a charge of 200 Arab cavalry was not something we did every day.

"Nothing?" Bernard asked incredulously.

"No, nothing. Iffen it were something, Lieutenant O'Bannon, he'd have ordered us to present arms again and fire. He never did, so it weren't nothing."

Chapter 41

Bomba, Libya
April 16, 1805

Jacob

We finally crested the ridge overlooking the ancient, abandoned port city of Bomba, eager for food, and saw…nothing. No ships, no sails. Nothing. Just blue water. I cannot begin to describe the utter feeling of dejection. Even our indomitable leader, General Eaton, looked deflated. Each of the sheiks came forward, demanding time with the spyglass, as if they could spot something the rest had missed.

Their anger grew, and they started calling the general "imposter" and "infidel," someone who had led them into a trap. They would not believe that any ships had even been there at all. But we had received reports, both from a messenger the general had sent forward and from two Bedouins we met on our march, that the ships had in fact been there at least until the day before.

The last stage of our march had started well enough. With two days of rest at the canyon where we had almost come to blows, the entire column had stepped off lively. This good mood did not last. At the first stop that next evening, we stopped at a cistern, and just as we started to draw the water, one of the Arabs jumped in and pulled out two dead men, apparently murdered. Fouled or not, we had to use the water.

The next day, at our stop, the general had the sacks of rice counted, and the number was obviously dire, as he only told the lieutenant the tally, and the lieutenant refused to let us know the number. The general ordered our rice rations cut in half to less than a handful. Not surprisingly, the sheiks did not take this well. Then, for the first time, Christians started to make noises of mutiny. The cannoneers were planning to take the remainder of the food by force of arms, and only after the general asked

Lieutenant Rocco to "gently" request that they reconsider (on pain of execution) was this threat averted. Luckily, the messenger arrived back at camp with word of the ships at Bomba, thus averting an ugly situation.

We were down to two rations of rice, not enough to reach Bomba, and then Hamet Bashaw took ill. We were forced to stop, and the next-to-last ration of rice was issued. Fortuitously, the bashaw began to feel better, so the next day, the forty-second of our march, we managed 25 miles, spurred on by visions of food awaiting us. We received the last of our rice, but with no firewood, we had to eat it uncooked.

It was as if the previous day's march had taken what few reserves we possessed. We only made seven-and-a-half miles, and the general, knowing we could not move on, convinced the Arabs to kill a camel and the Bedouins a sheep. There was meat and fat enough for everyone, but that did little to restore our strength or spirits. The Bedouins ate not only the meat and fat, though. They rendered down the beasts, consuming sinew, saving the hide for shoes, and cracking the bones for the marrow.

Pushing with the last ounces of our strength, we covered the last 25 miles to Bomba, buoyed by the reports of the two Bedouins that the ships were waiting for us. It was almost a physical blow when we finally arrived to find our ships gone.

The Mahomatens had a council, and they informed the general that they would be returning to Egypt in the morn without the company of any Christians. General Eaton implored them to march on to Derne, but they refused to consider it.

The general gathered up the Christians and took us to the mountain that overlooked the harbor and ordered us to gather twigs, branches, and anything that would burn. We made a number of bonfires, and at the general's orders, kept them burning all night. At daybreak, our hopeful eyes scanned the horizon, but there were no sails in sight. The sea was barren.

Below us, we could see the bashaw's men and the Arabs breaking camp. They were about to attempt the long march back to Egypt. The bashaw's *casnadar*, Zaid, the same man who the bashaw had whacked with the flat of his scimitar the week before, climbed the mountain to say goodbye. As he scanned the horizon one last time, he noted a small speck of white amongst the bright blue of the sea. He pointed it out to the lieutenant, and together they watched. That caught our attention, and we looked as well. Before long, another speck joined it, and the specks of white coalesced into sails.

Lieutenant O'Bannon marched over to where the general was sitting, pulling him to his feet and giving him the glasses.

"The *Argus* and the *Hornet*, sir," was all he said.

Lieutenant Hull had spotted our fires.

Chapter 42

Derne, Libya
April 26, 1805

Jacob

"So that's Derne," Bernard remarked as we peered through the small trees that covered the mountain overlooking the city.

"Don't look impressive for all we've gone to get here," Edward added.

"It's impressive enough, ladies," Sergeant Campbell said. "See that howitzer by the palace? That's a 10-incher. The spies told the general that the governor's got 800 troops, and the other bashaw's army is about 1,000 strong and almost here. We need to take Derne 'fore they get here."

I dare say all of us felt relieved that we had made it to our destination, but also apprehensive. We had recovered much of our strength, eating and drinking for three days at Bomba. For me, who had eschewed spirits for so long to save my dollars, the brandy Lieutenant Hull had sent ashore was very much welcomed. Further lifting our spirits was when Lorenzo Abbate, or as the general called his personal servant, "Lewis," married a Bedouin girl, and the *Nautilus* provided a feast to fit the occasion. The general was in fine fettle for that.

Upon reaching Bomba, though, we had fully expected to be joined by 100 more Marines, as the general had told us. Instead, the commodore had issued orders that no Marines would be attached to the general. When Lieutenant O'Bannon had protested our detachment, Lieutenant Hull relented, assuming that the commodore meant *no more* Marines. Mr. Peck returned to the *Argus*, but Mr. Danielson, who was the general's stepson, and Mr. Mann, both midshipmen, joined our company once more.

The general had requested a number of cannonade along with powder and shot, but before we could receive any, the *Argus* took to sail, and we started our march to Derne. The march itself was much easier than the march to Bomba. The land was cultivated, and we had no problem finding water. A day out of Derne, however, the sheiks once again refused to proceed. General Eaton had to offer them $2,000, which they accepted.

Now, looking over the city, we watched laborers working on breastworks. They knew we were coming and seemed intent on keeping us from our goal. They out-gunned us and out-manned us. We knew the general was positive that we would prevail, but he had made arrangements before we left as to the disposal of his personal possessions should he fall.

I looked out to sea again, but there was still nothing in sight. We needed the three ships to provide fire for us, else I was not sure how we could win the coming battle.

Lieutenant O'Bannon came up to where we were preparing and said, "Private Brissey, the general has need of your services."

John looked at me, then made a circle with his thumb and fingers and rubbed his nose in the middle of the circle. The others sniggered, and I made sure to trod on his leg as I went to join the lieutenant.

The general had a fine hand himself, but he had taken it into his head that my hand was finer, and for certain documents, he felt history would look more kindly upon him if the documents had a better appearance. I walked up and sat down to where paper, ink, and a quill were waiting for me.

The general dictated a letter to the governor, Mustifa Bey, asking for a free passage through the city and promising him a position in Hamet Bashaw's new government. I had a small blot while I wrote, and I had to begin again as the general would accept no such blemish. I finished the letter and gave it to the general for his signature. A messenger was standing by, and he took it and rushed down the mountain and into the city.

I was given no order to return, so I decided to take that as permission to stay. I made myself small and sat back while the officers discussed tactics. In my observations during the course of my two enlistments, officers could not leave a subject alone. They had to talk about it, covering it from every possible angle. As a private, things were easier and much more efficient. The sergeant spoke, and we got it done.

About an hour later, the messenger made his way back up the hill. He was covered with sweat when he reached us and had to wipe his hands on his robes to dry them before handing the general the governor's reply.

The general read it silently, then handed it to his staff so each one could read it. I moved forward, and as Mr. Mann read it, I looked over his shoulder.

My head or yours. —Mustifa

It seemed as if our course was set.

Chapter 43

Derne
April 27, 1805

Jacob

We watched the longboat make its way back to the *Nautilus*, taking the huge fieldpiece with it. The big brass gun would have been welcomed, but with the 20-foot cliffs, we could not get it ashore. The general, ever aware of the approaching army, decided we could waste no more time and energy on it. He wanted to launch our attack today, so he ordered the quest abandoned. While we would be relying on the *Argus'* 24-pounder long guns, the *Nautilus'* 12-pound cannonades, and the *Hornet's* brass six-pounders, we would only have the one small fieldpiece of our own.

The general's plan was simple. The Navy would try to take out the shore batteries, then fire in support of our attack. Hamet and the sheiks would ride to the land-side of the city and take the old castle in the Mesreat district of the city, while we Christians would take the city, southeast at the Ban Mansur district, focusing on the battery at Raz el Martariz with its eight 9-pound guns. We Marines would lead the attack with the Greek infantry in support and the other Greeks, Maltese, and Sicilians manning our small fieldpiece.

We went back to our supplies, got out our dress uniforms, and changed. Linen utilities just wouldn't do for this. As I buttoned up my jacket, I felt a sense of pride coming over me. I think we all felt it. I looked at the others with a sense of camaraderie. Bernard caught my eye and rendered me a salute. I came to attention and returned it.

"Private Edward Steward, where's your button?" John asked.

I looked around to where John was pointing. Edward's bottom button was missing. I wasn't sure how that could be as we hadn't worn our uniforms but once or twice.

"Well, we have time. Sew on one of your spares," I told him.

"I don't think you understand, there, Reverend," John went on. "I would 'spect our good private has no spares."

Edward shrugged, his face turning red. I was still confused.

"Goodness, for an educated lad, you can be a cod's head. He traded his buttons, and I'm sure you can understand why."

Then it struck me. Back at the Bedouin encampment, there had been offers for buttons, even offers from the women.

"Iffen I donst make it back from this little fight, then at least I will leave this earth with warm memories of a warm and eager piece," Edward said, a smile on his face.

We laughed, then stiffened when the sergeant came up after he had undoubtedly heard what had been said. He looked at Edward, reached in his pocket, and took out one of his brass buttons. He handed it to the astonished Edward, then walked off. No yelling, no blustering. He didn't say a word.

James helped Edward sew the button on, then we checked our muskets carefully. Now all we had to do was wait for the command.

At 2:00 PM, we started our attack.

"This is it!" John said beside me, excitement evident in his voice.

I enjoyed John's pranks, even when I was their target. He kept our spirits high when the situation was dire. Yet, despite his lack of seriousness, I could want for no one better beside me. He was a formidable man, stalwart and steady.

Our fieldpiece opened up with grape, intended to sweep our enemy from the breastworks. The Tripolitans returned fire, but we suffered naught from it. The *Hornet* came in close, nigh even 100 yards from the shore batteries, pounding them with their six-pounders. The other two ships stayed further offshore as befitted their guns' greater range.

As we started to advance, we saw Hamet Bashaw's forces in full gallop, green banners fluttering as they rode into the undefended fort that was their objective. Our fieldpiece continued to fire at an impressive rate, sending grape crashing into the breastworks. I looked up to watch when something long and dark flew to shatter on a stone wall. It was the rammer. The gun crew had accidentally fired it away. Our fieldpiece went silent.

The general swore at this, but he would not halt our advance. We would have to rely on the ships. Out in the harbor, the brave *Hornet* stood within pistol shot, hammering at the defenses. A Tripolitan shot severed the halliard that held aloft our stars and stripes, and it fell to the deck. Our hearts fell for a moment, but an officer picked it up, and through musket fire, climbed back up to nail it to the masthead. We cheered our admiration of the man, even if we were too far away to identify him.

As we continued our advance, there was a huge explosion near the palace. The Tripolitan's largest gun, an ancient piece, had exploded. We could hear the Tripolitan's cries of despair.

The fight had taken an hour or so, and we were at the last small hilltop before the Tripolitan fort. In front of us was about 100 yards of an open area, then a low temporary parapet surrounding a small courtyard and earthenworks in front of the fort and adjoining buildings. Musket fire was hitting amongst us, and while it caused no injuries, it was disconcerting to the Greeks. They milled about, edging further back down the hill. Dave looked back at them as if he wanted to join them, but after looking up and seeing the lieutenant and the sergeant with the general calmly observing the fort, he took a deep breath and stayed put.

General Eaton conferred with Lieutenant O'Bannon, then came to a decision. He knew we could not stay in place. We had to charge. We prepared ourselves. I was nervous, to be sure, but also excited. What man does not wonder how he will react in such a situation? I vowed that I would bring no shame upon my name or the Marine Corps.

With bayonets fixed, we waited until the general stood up and shouted, "Charge!" as the Greek bugler sounded the order to charge as well.

I was up and running before I realized it. With the general at the fore with Lieutenant Eaton, Mr. Mann, and Mr. Farquhar, the seven of us were right behind. The Greeks and other mercenaries with Captain Ulovix and the Janissary Selim Comb followed us. We were screaming at the top of our lungs, a polyglot charge of half-a-dozen languages. A tremendous volley of musket fire rang out, and John stumbled and fell. I jumped over him and continued to rush forward. To my right, I saw Edward fall, and then Dave stumbled as well, but he tried to get up to continue on. We had to close with the enemy before they could reload. Then our bayonets would give us the advantage.

The Tripolitans evidently came to the same conclusion, as most of them turned to run, abandoning their posts as soon as we reached the parapet. A few still fought, and I saw the general spin around and fall. I looked back for a moment to see who could help him just as Bernard fell, but he immediately got back up and staggered forward. I couldn't stop my own charge, so I faced forward again and kept going.

The Tripolitans had cut loopholes into the fort's walls, and from these, a few men were still firing at us. I caught a glimpse of the lieutenant ramming his cutlass into one hole, bringing it back out red with blood. A musket went off right in front of me, the ball going I know not where, and without thinking, I lunged forward, just as in training, putting my bayonet into the hole. I couldn't see anything more than a vague shape, but I felt my bayonet skitter off bone and heard an agonizing cry. I pulled back my musket, then rushed to the door where the lieutenant had already entered. I rushed in just in time to see him fire his pistol, striking a turbaned Tripolitan in the face. I looked for a target.

Mr. Mann was engaged with a large Tripolitan, cutlass to scimitar, and I rushed to assist him when another Tripolitan ran out, obviously with the same frame of mind to help his countryman. I stopped, took a breath and let it half out. I squeezed the trigger of my Charleville and felt a thrill course through me when my target fell to the ground.

I spun around, eager for more, amazed at the blood lust that took over me. I was a good Christian man, a man raised and educated by the church, a family man, but all I wanted to do was to kill. There were no more targets, however. All the Tripolitans were dead, wounded, or had fled. The fort was now in the hands of Lieutenant O'Bannon, Mr. Mann, Mr. Farquhar, Sergeant Campbell, James, Bernard, five Greek soldiers with Captain Ulovix and Selim Comb, and one Private Jacob Brissey.

I was breathing hard, both from exertion and from excitement. Lieutenant O'Bannon looked around and then vaulted the stairs to the main building. Atop the ramparts, he took down the Tripolitan flag, letting it fall into the dust, then opened his jacket and took out the United States flag he had carried since Cairo. We all watched as he hoisted it up the flagpole. Fifteen stars in a field of blue, and 15 red and white stripes fluttered proudly in the afternoon breeze. Even up in the fort, we could hear cheers echoing up from the harbor.

One of the fort's guns was undamaged and ready to fire, abandoned by its gun crew. Sergeant Campbell seized it, calling for help. Several of us rushed forward, Greeks and Americans, and we swung the gun around to face the fleeing Tripolitans. The lieutenant jumped down from the top of the ramparts and gave the order to fire. The round knocked two of the Tripolitans off their feet, probably killing them. Again and again we loaded and fired, causing much havoc as the bashaw's Arabs took the palace and attacked our enemy. Under fire from our ships as well as their own gun, and with the bashaw's cavalry attacking, the local Tripolitans had no choice but to surrender.

Derne was ours.

Chapter 44

USS Argus
Derne Harbor
May 8, 1805

Jacob

"So how're the lasses in the city?" Edward asked, as he lay in his hammock on the *Argus*.

I was shocked to see how sallow my friend looked. His cheeks were sunken in, and his eyes reflected the pain he must be feeling. He had taken a musket ball in the belly, and it had nicked his spine. Right after the battle, the surgeon had told the general that Edward wouldn't last the night, but here he was, 12 days later, still breathing.

"All harridans, I must confess. Nothing like your ladies in Cairo or at the Bedouin encampment.

"Ah, just as well. I'm not sure I have any more buttons to trade. Not sure my sugar stick's up to a good clicket now, either."

"You'll be screwing again soon, I'm sure," I told him.

I looked around the sickbay. Edward was still there, along with a Maltese soldier and two Greeks. Dave Thomas had taken a ball in the leg, but he was back on shore now, assisting the work the best he could. Bernard had been hit in the side, but after surgery and two days aboard the *Argus*, he too had rejoined us back on shore.

I fingered the hole in my jacket, a habit to which I had taken. A ball had gone through it, but it had not touched me. A few inches to the left and I would have been pierced.

Edward was grievously, perhaps mortally wounded. Bernard had been hit, and Dave might limp for the rest of his mortal life. All told, 13 Christians, including the general himself, who had taken a ball through the wrist, had been wounded in our charge to take the fort. One soul had died: Private John Whitten.

I thought of him often as we toiled to build up the fort, building walls, digging entrenchments, setting in guns. I half expected to hear his jesting just when we needed it; and I half expected to bear the brunt of one of his pranks. But he had gone to meet his maker, taking a ball in the heart just as we began our charge.

This was my second trip back to the ship, and the first time, I thought that Edward would not last until I saw him again. I was gratified that he was still alive. I did not want to lose two friends for Hamet Bashaw.

A sailor poked his head in the compartment and said, "You needs to git to the longboat. Hassan Aga's army's come, and all going ashore needs to git ashore."

We had been expecting this, hence all the work we were doing to fortify the city. I looked down at Edward and grabbed his hand, giving it a squeeze. Somehow, the prospect of battle was not as exciting to me as it was before.

"Go on, Reverend. Leave a few for me, though. I'll be ashore to join you right soon enough," he said, before a fit of coughing cut him off.

"You better get ashore soon, you malingerer. It's not right that you let us do all the grunt work, then you get there just in time for the glory."

I turned away and rushed to the deck, ready to board the longboat. In the distance, I thought I could make out a gathering of horsemen to the southeast of the city, right where we had begun our own attack 12 days before.

Chapter 45

Derne
May 12, 1805

Jacob

General Eaton gave one last look at us, adjusted the sling that held his left hand in place, then turned and marched out of Fort Enterprise, as we now called our emplacement at Raz el Martariz. Mr. Danielson was at his side, and we Marines—the lieutenant, the sergeant, and James, Bernard, Dave, and I—followed next and were in turn followed by 40 Greeks with Selim Comb at their head.

The general had no more time to give Mustifa Bey, who had taken refuge in his harem. Two days prior, he had asked the sheik of Mesreat, where the harem was located, to turn over Mustifa, but the old man refused. Although loyal to Hamet Bashaw, he said all custom forbade him to turn out anyone dependent on his hospitality. For two days, the general stewed, remarking to all that Mustifa was now a prisoner of war and did not deserve the niceties of a harem. Now, the general was determined to take the bey into custody.

We marched down from the fort and into the city. At first, the locals paid us little heed, but as we approached Mesreat and the harem, they became agitated, calling out to each other. We arrived at the harem where the old sheik greeted us. After the general loudly proclaimed his intent to take the bey, dead or alive, the sheik calmly stated that he would not surrender his guest.

I took a quick glance around. People were gathering, none too pleased, where before they gave us a degree of nonchalance. I shifted my hands on my musket, ready to move into action.

Hamet Bashaw arrived at that moment, and he pleaded with the general that we would cause an insurrection, and with Hassan Aga's forces in the heights, this could undo all that had heretofore been accomplished. Much to my surprise, the general backed down and ordered us back to the fort.

There were consequences to this action, though. During the night, Mustifa Bey "escaped" the harem and joined Hassan Aga. This was enough to move the commander to begin the attack we had so long expected. At five o'clock the next morning, Hassan Aga's army was formed for the attack, five green standards fluttering in the breeze.

Between the enemy and the town was a detachment of Hamet's cavalry, but only 100 men to face Hassan Aga's more than 1,000. For the next several hours, we waited for the enemy to make their move. This delay, though, gave the *Argus* and *Hornet* time to move into position to help repel the attack. Finally, just before nine o'clock, the Tripolitans urged their mounts forward and began to flow into the town.

We watched the first riders reach Hamet's outpost, and while those soldiers put up a good fight, they could not stand against the odds. They fell back, and the two ships joined our own pieces to pour fire into the advancing army. A party of men from Mesreat rushed forward, and more than a few of us suspected treachery, but it was soon clear that they had joined up with Hamet Bashaw's forces. Despite this, the Hamet's cavalry was pushed back and many were driven out into the trees surrounding the town. Others were forced into the palace courtyard where they would have to make a stand.

The general paced back and forth, obviously agitated as he conferred with the lieutenant and Mr. Farquhar. If Hamet fell, then all our efforts would have been for naught.

We could clearly see from our vantage point when the first of Hassan Aga's cavalry rode into the courtyard. Just as clearly, we could see them struck down dead by a 24-pound shell fired by the *Argus*. The gruesome and sudden nature of their deaths struck deep into the attackers' fortitude. Within moments, a few broke and ran. This was like a dam being swept away. After the first few ran, others joined them, and shortly, the entire enemy army was in full flight.

We continued to fire on them as they fled out of the city and up the heights. With Hamet Bashaw's forces taking the heaviest part of the fight, we had pushed back the enemy. We had 14 killed, none of them being amongst the Christians. Hassan Aga's forces lost 39 men, killed or mortally wounded to die later.

Chapter 46

Tripoli
May 24, 1805

Ichabod

I had just spent the day in the boat yard, hauling timbers, and my body ached fiercely. I didn't even want to eat, but I dragged myself to where Justice Meeker had boiled up a weak soup. I held out my bowl just as Mr. Cowdery came into our midst.

Mr. Cowdery had the ear of the bashaw, and he became our only source of news, our own town crier. He looked excited.

"Our forces, under Mr. Eaton, have taken Derne and put Sidi Hamet on the throne," he told us as we gathered. "The bashaw is sore worried."

Several sailors let out a "huzzah!" but others of us looked worried.

"And what about us? Will the bashaw order us killed?" William Ray asked, putting to words what most of us feared.

"Ah, yes, there is that," Mr. Cowdery replied. "The bashaw has indeed threatened us with death, but today he didn't mention anything of the sort. I didn't think it prudent to ask him about that, reminding him of that dastardly option. You don't know him, but he is not a monster. He is a rational man, and I think he could not stoop so low."

"Not a monster?" William countered. "Who but a monster would keep us here as slaves for nigh on 570 days of misery? Who else but Satan himself?"

There were mutters of agreement. I was surprised. I had not been keeping track, but it had been 570 days? It seemed like a lifetime ago that I had been a free man, a man in charge of my own destiny.

Mr. Cowdery took a step back in the face of William's anger. William might be a small man, but the truth in his accusation carried weight, methinks.

"Certainly, I did not mean to imply less. I am just giving my opinion now that we will be safe and sound. The bashaw confided to me that if it is in his power, he will accept peace and let us go. Pray to the Lord Almighty, and our servitude will be over soon," he said before turning and taking his leave.

"I've prayed and prayed, but right now, I think I would rather pray that this Mr. Eaton will soon be marching through the gates of this accursed city," Achilles offered after Mr. Cowdery had left.

In some ways, I felt the same, but the ever-present threat of execution was a pall cast over any hopes of rescue.

Chapter 47

Derne
May 27, 1805

Jacob

"Thirty dollars? I wouldn't give a silver dime for you, Private Thomas," Bernard said with a laugh. "The Reverend here though, he's got the general's eye, so he could be worth it."

The sirocco raged outside, and even in our small room, with the door closed and a blanket nailed up against it, sand still made its way in. All of us were covered in a fine tan coating, barely distinguishable from each other. The storm had buffeted us for nigh on four days with only one small respite.

"I'm worth more than you, I dare say," Dave gave back at him. "Least I can still do a man's work with a ball in my leg."

The change in Dave had been significant since we took Derne. He had always been a pessimist, always complaining, and we feared somewhat of a coward. He proved us wrong in Derne, taking a ball to the leg, but still trying to fight on. After getting it cut out, he refused light duty, but demanded to be treated like any other able-bodied Marine.

Bernard, on the other hand, had stayed on the *Argus* for two days to recover from the ball that had struck his side, going in and out at the same time.

"With you two prattling on and on like fishwives, any Arab could find us in this storm, reach in, and drag you out to collect his reward," James said.

"I'd like to see any one of them try it," Dave replied with a snort. "Not that those hectors would dare. I'd stick 'em with my steel," he told us, brandishing his bayonet.

When we heard that there was a $30 bounty on our heads for anyone who could deliver said heads, attached to the rest of us or not, to Hassan Aga, it was sobering at first. But quickly, we took it as a badge of honor. Sure, the general had a $6,000 bounty on his head, $12,000 if he was still alive, but even Lieutenant O'Bannon had the same $30 on his head.

"I'd watch Constantine if I were you. He's liable to lure you off into the woods, then turn you in for the reward. He's been eyeing you keenly lately," Bernard told Dave.

Constantine was a Greek private. He'd always seem fascinated with us, and with his broken English, he felt it was his duty to be our point of contact with the rest of the mercenaries. He'd been at the fore during our charge to take Derne and had accounted for two Tripolitans, for all he looked like he'd have problems defeating a kitten. After the battle, he had been in awe of Dave's wounded leg, and how Dave refused to step down from his duties. He'd come to our small quarters several times with food cooked in the Greek style, offering it first to Dave, then to the rest of us. We joked that Constantine had taken a more prurient interest in our friend, even if we knew it wasn't true.

"At least he can cook. Mayhaps I'd rather have him around than you lollpoop bastards!"

I looked around at the other three. Edward was still on the *Argus*, in dire condition, but still breathing. John was gone, and we all missed him. Yet the four of us had a bond that couldn't be broken. I still thought of Ichabod and Seth, and I longed to see them, but the bonds of battles fought were special. We were Marines, but we were more than that. We were brothers.

Jonathan P. Brazee

Chapter 48

Derne
May 28, 1805

Jacob

The sirocco broke the afternoon before, and we spent the afternoon cleaning ourselves and oiling our weapons. Four days of confinement had left us with extra energy, and we almost looked forward to action.

I think the general felt the same. Midmorning, Hassan Aga sent a raiding party of 60 foot soldiers and some cavalry to raid one of the Bedouin encampments at the edge of town. They drove off some sheep, but then Hamet Bashaw himself led his men in pursuit, regaining the livestock. Hassan Aga's raiding party turned towards the shore to escape.

We had been observing this from Fort Enterprise, and when the enemy turned, General Eaton quickly called us to arms. With Mr. Mann, Mr. Farquhar, and a dozen Greeks, the six Marines, and I include the lieutenant and sergeant in that small number, followed the general as we ran pell-mell down from the fort to cut off their retreat. We barely interposed ourselves between them and their main encampment before they made their appearance, much shocked by finding us there waiting for them.

They may have been shocked, but quickly they brought up their muskets just as we fired, firing their own volley. General Eaton did not wait. Immediately upon discharging our muskets, he ordered us to charge. Once again, the Marines led the charge, screaming as we lowered our bayonets and closed the distance. Not one of our enemy finished reloading his own musket. Every one of them turned and fled. We pursued, quickly catching up to them. I saw Bernard thrust his bayonet into the neck of their fleeing captain, dropping him like a sack of rice. I lunged forward at another, but in my lunge, my bayonet fell from where I intended to strike his back, and my steel went deep into his buttocks. He fell with a horrible screech and twisted to look back at me, hands raised in fear or supplication. I am not sure why I didn't finish him instead of just kicking his side as I rushed forward. Our officers fired their pistols, and I saw one turbaned Tripolitan fling up his arms from a ball in the back before falling to the dirt.

We heard the beat to arms from the camp in front of us, and our charge faltered and came to a stop. I was breathing hard, wondering if the sand from the sirocco had somehow lodged in my lungs, robbing me of my breath. I held up my musket so that the bayonet caught the morning sun, red from the tip to about six inches down its length.

Suddenly, about 200 cavalry trotted up to us, halting outside of musket range. With General Eaton's arm still in a sling, we didn't have his rifle, so we had nothing that could reach them.

We caught our breath and looked at our foe, waiting for their charge. With 20 of us, we wouldn't stand a chance if they attacked. I looked over at Bernard for a moment, wondering if it was finally our time.

"Fall back slowly, but keep facing them," the general ordered.

Step by step, we backed up, keeping a united front facing them. To this day, I wonder why they let us go, why they didn't charge. The general remarked later that they must have thought we were leading them into a trap. I'm not so sure. While they could have overrun us, we most certainly would have taken many of them with us, and from what our spies told us, morale in their camp was low. Hadji Ismain Bey, their treasurer and second-in-command, has just deserted, along with their payroll, and their complete lack of success against us was most demoralizing. I think that without pay, without their hearts in the fight, no one was willing to become the sacrificial lamb in order to defeat our small group.

We made it back without incident, having killed five of them, wounding at least six others, and capturing two. I saw the man I had bayoneted drag himself to the side as we passed, and for once, I didn't regret his continued existence on this earth. I knew we had a fierce task ahead of us in taking Tripoli and rescuing our prisoners, but for now, one less death by my hands was acceptable.

Jonathan P. Brazee

Chapter 49

USS Argus
Derne Harbor
May 30, 1805

Jacob

Private Edward Thomas, United States Marine Corps, met his maker this morning. His body could not fight the corruption any longer, and he just gave up. We received the message at about 8 o'clock, and I think it hit us all hard. We had been expecting it, but the longer Edward kept fighting, the more we thought he could pull through.

Several sailors stayed at the fort to stand sentry while the six Marines took a longboat out to the *Argus*. Silently, we made our way to sickbay. Edward had been laid out on the surgeon's table, dressed in only his linens. Some say that there is peace in death, but Edward did not look like he went easily. His face was etched in pain and despair. I could only hope he was now at the hand of our Lord, all suffering gone.

The sailors had taken care laying him out, and his uniform was folded neatly beside him. They realized that this was a task that we had to do. We carefully dressed him, polishing his brass and making sure he looked his best. His body had not yet gone stiff, so we had no problem getting his uniform on him. When we were finished, we stepped back, taking one last look at our friend. We put the canvas shroud under him, along with the lead weights, but before we started to sew it up, James pulled the bottom button off his jacket, then put it in Edward's pocket. Without a word being spoken, the rest of us pulled a button off as well, adding them to the one James had given. Lieutenant O'Bannon looked at Sergeant Campbell with a questioning look. He wasn't there with us before our fight, so he didn't realize the significance of our action.

Nevertheless, he stepped forward, ripped off one of his officer's buttons, and placed it in Edward's pocket as well.

That done, we sewed the shroud closed. James, Bernard, and I lifted Edward's body and carried him onto the main deck. Lieutenant Hull and the chaplain were there along with the rest of the *Argus'* Marines. Quickly, sailors stopped their tasks and came to stand at formation. I am not sure what the chaplain said. His words never registered with me. Eventually, though, he finished. The drummer and fifer played, and we consigned our friend to the sea's embrace.

Chapter 50

Derne
June 1, 1805

Jacob

General Eaton looked like a beaten man after the *Hornet* sailed into port the afternoon before. Instead of supplies and money, though, the letter from Commodore Barron had informed the general that no more funds were to be made available for Hamet Bashaw's forces, and even the supplies the *Hornet* delivered were to only be used by Christians.

I expected him to rail at this, but he merely spoke aloud to Lieutenant O'Bannon, Mr. Mann, Jean Eugene, and Mr. Farquhar, asking their opinions. He even spoke to James and to me, as if we were gentlemen as well. His feeling was that if we stopped supporting Hamet, his people would be massacred, and all the good we had done would be lost. He had more than a few unkind words for Mr. Lear, the Consul General, calling him some names I would prefer not repeat now, but for most of the evening, he was more morose.

This morning, though, he was a renewed man. Calling his officers before him, he explained that he would not give up Derne until he received specific orders to do so. He vowed to keep the city. He requested Hamet Bashaw's presence and told him what the commodore had written, but Hamet took it rather well, I thought, as if he had been expecting this turn of events.

On our long march across the desert, I thought the bashaw to be weak and unable to lead. I felt he was a coward, and I wondered if he could ever head Tripoli. However, as I watched him lead men into battle, my opinion changed. His personal courage never faltered, and his men willingly followed him. No one was going to ask a mere private of Marines, but I thought he might be able to perform his duties admirably.

Later that afternoon, the bashaw and a small retinue of men returned to Fort Enterprise and sought out Lieutenant O'Bannon. The four of us stood at attention behind Sergeant Campbell as the bashaw approached the lieutenant. They stood face to face, and the bashaw spoke quietly to him for a few moments, too quiet for us to hear what was said. The bashaw turned, and one of his men handed him a curved saber in the style of the Mamelukes. He presented this to Lieutenant O'Bannon, who took it and saluted him. Both men shook hands in the Western manner.

As the bashaw moved off to seek out the general, Lieutenant O'Bannon made an about face and dismissed us. From the expression on his face, I felt that perhaps his opinion of the bashaw might have changed just as mine had.

He strode off to the small room he had appropriated as his quarters. Moments later, the strains of Master Johann Sebastian Bach floated off his fiddle and out over the fort.

Chapter 51

Tripoli
June 4, 1805

Ichabod

I could barely walk, but nothing was going to stop me. In front of me was a longboat, ready to take me to the *Essex*. After 579 days, we were free.

We had first gotten wind that peace was almost at hand two days ago, on Sunday. Still, our drivers came to take us to work, and some of us attempted to refuse, only to suffer another bastmanding. We went to work.

Upon returning to our jail that evening, Mr. Cowdery came once again, but this time with Captain Bainbridge hisself, who told us that peace was near and that we should not let the prospect of freedom "transport us beyond the bounds of discretion." As we had previously discussed, we gave a letter to the captain, asking him to dock our salaries to raise $300 for Giovani Milano, the Neapolitan slave of Captain Blackbeard, a man who had treated us kindly during our imprisonment. After he left, Mr. Cowdery made mention that the plans we had made to fight if our day of execution arrived would not have to be enacted.

Some of the men had spirits, and most of us took liberal amounts of it. I dare say a goodly number of us were cup-shot that night and into the morning. Force of habit made us get up, but our drivers never arrived. We remained locked up until nigh on 10 o'clock, a true sign that we would soon be free. Once our doors were unlocked, we were not put to work but rather left to our own devices. Our own devices meant buying food and spirits with what money we had amongst us.

For once, we were willingly locked back into our jail that evening. We continued to drink and sing until morning, when we were told that the peace treaty had been signed the night before. Our government was paying

Yusef Hamet $60,000 and releasing all Tripolitan prisoners. William Ray noted that was about $277 apiece for each of us.

During the evening, the bashaw called up our five turks who put on the turban, them being John Wilson, William Smith, Lewis Hexiner, Stephen West, and Thomas Prince. He told them we Americans were being freed and our turks could go home if they wanted. Only Wilson said he liked being a Mahomaten, that he wanted to stay. This was a ruse, of course, and the other three were sent into the desert. We saw them being marched by our door looking sore afeerd, with West and Hexiner calling back for our help, and we have nary seen them since.

When our doors were unlocked for the last time, we stumbled out of our jail. I was feeling both the utter joy of freedom as well as the headache of too much to drink. I was still a mite cup-shot, truth be told, and if I was unsteady on my feet, I was not alone. Let our countrymen assume we were in this condition 'cause of our treatment. But it is not often that a man walks free after so long, and I didn't regret each cup of date palm spirit or wine we drank through the night.

I half-expected someone to shout for us to halt, that there had been a mistake. I kept looking back, ready to run if I saw armed men chasing us. But we made it to the boats without incident, and as I stepped down into the longboat, its rocking made me stumble again.

Afore too long, we were loaded, and the tars pulled hard at their oars. The *Essex* was at anchor, and I think I ne'er seen such a beautiful sight. We pulled alongside and helpful hands assisted us up the ladders. I clamored over the rails and stood on a capital ship of the United States Navy. Only then did I finally feel I was delivered.

I fell to the deck of that lovely ship and cried.

Jonathan P. Brazee

Chapter 52

Derne
June 11, 1805

Jacob

"The war is over, and our prisoners have been freed," Lieutenant Wederstrandt shouted to the general as he made his way into the fort. He had just come from the *Constellation*, which had sailed into Derne two hours ago.

"Are you mad, sir? Hold your tongue unless you want to see us all massacred," the general reprimanded him.

He took the letters the lieutenant gave him, then went to his small quarters to read them alone. I looked at Sergeant Campbell and gave a slight shrug. If peace was at hand, then what would become of Hamet Bashaw's men? Had the Tripolitans accepted him as their rightful leader?

Just the day before, Hamet Bashaw, with his 2,000 cavalry, had defeated a force of 3,000 men under Hassan Aga in a fierce battle over a period of four hours. While the *Argus'* guns undoubtedly were of service, the bulk of the fighting was conducted by Hamet's men. Lieutenant O'Bannon had wanted to rush into the fray, but General Eaton had forbidden it. Hamet Bashaw won the day with his own forces.

If we had any thoughts of Hamet Bashaw being the new ruler of Tripoli, those were dashed when the general returned, livid and red in the face. He cursed those above us, and he especially cursed "Aunt Lear," who he accused of sabotage, a political worm who cared naught for honor and righteousness but only for his own accolades.

He called in his officers and told them what had transpired. He dismissed the treaty, saying, "We gave a kingdom for peace.

"The war is over, men, over too soon. We have this city of 12,000 in our control, but Commodore Rodgers now orders us to stand down, to leave Derne and offer no more assistance to our allies.

Still angry, he ordered us to keep quiet, for word of this could spell our deaths. He retired to his room to contemplate what he wanted to do. Lieutenant Wederstrandt left for the *Constellation* while we returned to our quarters.

As I stood sentry duty that night, I wondered what our general would do. For once, I was glad to be only a private, without such heavy considerations weighing me down.

Chapter 53

Derne
June 12, 1805

Jacob

General Eaton inspected us one last time. We stood proudly in formation, six Marines, 38 Greeks, and 42 artillerymen. The general had given word to prepare for a major attack on the coming morn, and we had spent the day cleaning our weapons and sharpening blades. Both Sergeant Campbell and I, however, knew this was only a ruse. I had come to this conclusion on my own, given the letters the general had received, and when I had quietly asked the sergeant, he merely told me to keep silent and tell no one else.

The general didn't say anything, but he seemed in a contemplative mood. He sent out a few patrols around 8 o'clock, but that would be normal before a battle. He also gave orders to divest ourselves of any unneeded equipment we might have obtained.

Around midnight, the Greeks were given orders to quietly leave the fort and move down to the waterfront. This still made sense as they could be moving to a new assault position. We Marines were ordered to act as if we were on sentry duty, marching back and forth along Fort Enterprise's ramparts. Even Sergeant Campbell took his position as if he was a lowly private.

Instead of moving to an assault position, the Greeks were loaded into the *Constellation's* longboats that were waiting on the wharfs. To give them credit, some of the men balked, not willing to abandon our allies, but they were quieted and made to board the boats.

The boats took about two hours to reach the ship, then another two hours to return. At midnight, the general sent a message to the bashaw, asking for his presence. This was a pre-arranged signal. The bashaw and 40 of his men arrived and loaded directly into the longboats.

We lowered the American flag that had flown so proudly over the fort, the first American flag to fly over foreign soil. It was a solemn occasion, and not a word was spoken. James handed the folded flag to Sergeant Campbell, and the sergeant gave it to Lieutenant O'Bannon.

While we were doing that, Mr. Mann, Mr. Farquhar, and Jean Eugene reached and boarded the boats. We marched down and filed on board as well. Lieutenant O'Bannon silently handed the flag to the general and joined us.

General Eaton looked at us, then turned back to look at the city, maybe thinking of opportunities lost. He shook his head, then stepped on board as the sailors put their oars in the water and pulled away from the wharf.

We had hardly gone beyond pistol shot when the wharf erupted with shouts and the firing of weapons. The citizens of Derne had discovered our deception. We had abandoned them, and our war was over. Theirs was not. We had defeated the Tripolitans at every turn, yet in the end we had paid a ransom for peace.

1805-1850

The treaty ending the war with Tripoli was signed on June 3, 1805. The treaty stipulated that all prisoners held by either side would be released, the United States would pay Tripoli $60,000, and the United States would evacuate all personnel from Derne. A secret part of the treaty was added, which stipulated that Yusef Pasha would keep his brother's wife and children hostage for at least four more years to ensure Hamet Qaramanli would not foment any further rebellions.

Indications prior to Tobias Lear's negotiations were that the pasha was willing to accept no payments in order to achieve peace; however, Mr. Lear had made comments about allowing the pasha to save face, so it is possible that this payment was for this purpose.

Reports came from the Antoine Zuchet, the Counsel from the Republique Batave (Holland under Napoleonic rule), that upon the departure of the Americans, Yusef Pasha raged against his subjects, personally punishing those he deemed fit. In Derne a large number of prominent citizens disappeared, never to be heard from again. This justified Eaton's concern about abandoning those who had fought for the American cause.

Hamouda Pasha, the Tunisian leader, was not pleased with the Tripolitan treaty. He threatened war, so Commodore Rodgers, who had been planning an assault in Tripoli, sailed all 18 ships of the squadron in mid-July into the harbor at Tunis and demanded a separate treaty. He had it by the next day.

In 1807, the British enacted a series of trade restrictions, which were designed to keep the United States from trading with France, with whom the British were at war. Tensions mounted further when the British Navy impressed British-born sailors serving on American ships. Americans became incensed with the Leander Affair as well with the *USS Chesapeake* surrendering to the *HMS Leopard*. On June 1, 1812, President Madison asked Congress for a declaration of war.

Emboldened by the war with Britain, the Barbary States began to take American shipping once again. It wasn't until 1815, after peace was declared between the United States and Britain, that the United States could divert military power to address the problem. Commodore Stephen Decatur sailed with a force of ten ships. Capturing two Algerian ships on the passage, Decatur sailed into Algiers harbor during the last week of June. Decatur demanded a cessation of seizing foreign shipping, a release of all prisoners, and $10,000 recompense for the previous seizure of American vessels. After some hesitation, the bey capitulated, and the treaty was signed on July 3, 1815.

Lieutenant Presley Neville O'Bannon served in the Marines until 1807, when he resigned because he could not get promoted to captain. He returned to Virginia, and in 1809, he moved to Kentucky with his wife and had a son, Eaton, who died as an infant. He served in both houses of the Kentucky legislature and died on September 12, 1850.

In 1812, the Virginia legislature awarded him a Sword of Virginia. The sword was designed by John Carter and was a saber patterned after the one given to him by Hamet Qaramanli. The sword was presented in the fall of that year in what is now Alexandria, Virginia. From 1791 to 1846, Alexandria was part of the District of Columbia.

In Frankfurt, a memorial in his honor was erected with the inscription:

> *As Captain of the United States Marines, he was the First to Plant the American Flag on Foreign Soil.*

In 1825, Archibald Henderson, the Commandant of the Marine Corps, ordered that all officers carry a sword patterned after the one presented to Lieutenant O'Bannon by the Virginia legislature. The sword was referred to as a "Mameluke," after the Arabs troops who carried swords in this style.

William Eaton returned to the United States a hero. He attempted several times to be appointed a military attaché, but his requests fell on deaf ears, probably due to his continual haranguing of members of Congress to support Hamet Qaramanli and to denigrate Tobias Lear's actions.

Eaton had spent $29,108 of his own funds in his mission. Congress waited a year, then paid him $12,636.60. In 1807, the people of Brimfield, Massachusetts voted him into the state legislature. Prior to taking his seat, he stood as a witness in the trial of Aaron Burr over the dueling death of Alexander Hamilton. After serving one term, he was not re-elected.

Bored, depressed, and with his war injuries causing him pain, he took to drinking more often. In July of 1808, he received news that his stepson, Eli Danielson, had been killed in a duel with another naval officer. In addition to his war injuries, he now began to suffer from gout and rheumatism.

William Eaton died on June 1, 1811.

Tobias Lear remained as Consul General to the Barbary States until war broke out in 1812. He returned to the Unites States, but instead of the honored position he had envisioned, he was somewhat vilified in the press for his conduct in the treaty with Tripoli. Thomas Jefferson, his erstwhile protector, disavowed any knowledge of the "secret treaty" concerning Hamet Qaramanli's family. On October 11, 1816, he committed suicide by shooting himself in the head with his pistol.

Lear is also noted in history for his part of the missing Washington papers. Upon Washington's death in 1799, Lear, who had partnered with Washington in a business venture, took possession of the president's papers. When he released them a year later, six vital letters and almost all diary entries were missing. The missing papers were thought to record derogatory information concerning Thomas Jefferson. Lear denied the destruction of any of the papers; however, in a letter to Alexander Hamilton, he had offered to do just that.

On March 22, 1820, Commodore Decatur was killed in a duel with Commodore James Barron. Their enmity had never cooled since Decatur's less-than-flattering comments about Barron's older brother, Commodore Samuel Barron, while in Syracuse following the signing of the treaty with Tripoli in 1805. The situation was further exacerbated when Decatur sat on the board of Barron's court martial in 1807 for losing his ship, the *USS Chesapeake*, to the British.

Captain William Bainbridge, who was Decatur's second in his duel with Barron, continued to serve in the Navy as commander of several Navy yards. He died on July 8, 1833.

Commodore Edward Preble helped design ships and gunboats for the Navy until his death on August 25, 1807.

Jean Eugene (Gervasio Santuari/ Lieutenant Leitensdorfer) continued his colorful life. He wandered the world until 1809, when he visited Eaton and obtained a letter of recommendation. With that in hand, he got a job with Benjamin Henry Latrobe, Jefferson's chief architect, as a surveyor of public buildings. In 1833, he was granted 320 acres in Missouri for his part in the Battle of Derne. He died on his land in 1845.

Hamet Qaramanli went to Egypt after Derne. Thanks to Eaton's perseverance, he was awarded an appropriation of $2400 and a $200 monthly stipend from the United States. He was united with his family after the secret terms of the treaty concerning his family were made public. He returned to take the position of governor of Derne in 1809, but fled back to Egypt to save his life in 1811. No records are known as to the time or circumstances of his death.

Yusef Pasha remained on the throne until 1835. With his sons squabbling over succession, the British asked the Turks to intervene, and Nejib Pasha took over, evicting the Qaramanli family from the throne. Yusef died in 1837.

Jonathan P. Brazee

Epilogue

Washington DC
September, 1812

Jacob

"So this must be the famous Suva Brissey," a familiar voice rang out behind me.

I turned to see a short, broad-shouldered Marine sergeant come to the gate. He nodded at the sentry, who then opened it. We entered, and the sergeant pounded my back.

"This is a right treat, I thinks," Sergeant Seth Crocker said as he looked me over.

We hadn't seen each other since July of 1806, when I left to return to Princeton and my wife. In the meantime, he had learned to read and had been promoted to sergeant. He looked good.

The Marine barracks had changed. Several new buildings were up, and it no longer had the look of raw construction. There was also a sense of urgency. With war declared on the British, these Marines would soon sail into harm's way once again.

"And who's this?" he asked, bending over to look at my son, who was clutching Suva's skirt, in awe of the Marine in front of us.

"That's Presley, my son. Presley, say hello to Sergeant Crocker."

Presley had other ideas. He took a step back, using Suva's skirt as a shield.

"Ah, no matter. I'm guessing he'll be a Marine hisself, soon enough." He looked back at me. "I was surprised to gets your letter. I mean you coming all the way from New Jersey and all. Ichabod's already here, at the boarding house on I Street. I can walks you over there, but then I has to be back here for the night. Tomorrow, I gots a carriage to bring us there."

174

Seth took us down the block to where a boarding house had a room waiting under my name. Ichabod wasn't in his room, but he had arrived the day before. Seth made his goodbyes and left to return to the barracks.

"Well, I must say, he's exactly as you described him," Suva said. "Isn't he a bit, well, rough, to be a sergeant?"

"He taught himself to read well enough to get by, and if you spoke to anyone who has served with him, you would not doubt his abilities."

"I'm sure you're right, but he just doesn't seem to be much of a gentleman."

I let it go. Suva was my love and the mother of my pride and joy, but she would never understand the feelings of soldiers, feelings that we probably had back to Alexander. Seth was a man I would trust with my life.

It was late, and we'd been travelling by coach for two long days. Dinner would be served soon, so I let Presley play on the floor while I went to look for Ichabod and Bernard. I stepped outside and looked into the first tavern. As expected, both men were there, both deep into their cups.

"Reverend!" Bernard shouted as I made my entrance.

Both men bounded to their feet to give my back a pounding. I felt overjoyed to see the two of them. I accepted the proffered seat and the mug of beer. Leaning back in my stool, I took both of them in.

If anything, Ichabod looked thinner than before. I think the long time spent in the bashaw's dungeon had made its mark, and I doubt he would ever overcome it. What little hair he had left was a light grey. His eyes still had that sparkle I knew so well, though.

We had both spent our last year at the barracks right here, and the routine had been welcome. Bernard was sent to the Boston Navy Yard, but not before I introduced him to Seth and Ichabod. Unfortunately, Bernard's wound had festered, and he had been discharged.

Dave was still a Marine, still a private, serving aboard the *United States*, which had already put to sea. James was a corporal on my old ship, the *Argus*. It would have been great had the two been here as well, but duty called.

We talked about everything and nothing through the evening and once again after dinner. They were interested in my new life as a trader. General Eaton's letter of recommendation got me a position with a small trading company in Philadelphia after I mustered out, and that grew until I was able to buy out the owner when he retired the year past. Bernard had a position with the Massachusetts state legislature, another position acquired thanks to the auspices of the general. Ichabod, well, Ichabod had held a variety of positions, even a year as a sailor on the *Chesapeake*, back when the *HMS Leopard* forced her to surrender. I wonder if perhaps he was bad luck to seafaring folk.

It was after midnight when I crept back into my room. Suva was asleep already, Presley cradled before her. I quietly slid into bed behind her and fell asleep.

In the morning, we woke early, made our toilet, and went down to breakfast. Ichabod and Bernard were there already, and I made introductions. Right at 8 o'clock, Seth showed up with the carriage. We loaded up and started our trip to Alexandria.

I enjoyed taking in the sights. Washington had changed over the last five years. It was beginning to look more like a real city. Government buildings were being built, and the city began to have its own flavor.

In Philadelphia, the trees were already beginning to turn, but here in the capital, summer was holding on for a few last moments. It was not hot, but it was comfortably warm. Our carriage crossed the Long Bridge, which hadn't been built yet when I was still stationed in the city. This made crossing easier than taking a ferry.

Alexandria had been part of Virginia before being annexed as part of the District of Columbia in 1791, the only part of old Virginia to be part of the federal district. It was a picturesque, pretty town, and Suva was quite taken with it. We slowly made our way to the old courthouse and dismounted the carriage. It was 9 o'clock.

At once, I saw a familiar, tall figure. I started to walk toward him when he turned and spied me. With four or five long strides, he reached me and stuck out his hand. I happily took it. It seemed odd to see him in civilian clothes, but Lieutenant (for that is how I will always remember him) Presley O'Bannon still had the demeanor and stature of a Marine officer.

"Well, Reverend, I am most pleased to see you again. I trust the years have been good to you?"

I was surprised that he used my nickname from the March to Derne. I had never heard him utter it before.

"And is that my jig partner?" he asked as Bernard reached us.

Bernard did a few steps of the jig in answer and we all laughed. I introduced Suva and Presley. When he heard little Presley's name, a tear appeared momentarily in his eye as he solemnly bent over to shake my son's hand. I had heard that the lieutenant had just lost his own small son, so I didn't know what to say.

A clerk came up and told us the ceremony was about to begin. We followed the lieutenant and his wife Matilda into an ornate room where several important-looking men stood along with a number of Marines in full dress, including Lieutenant Colonel Wharton, the Commandant. I just wished that General Eaton would have been able to come, God rest his soul.

A young-looking man with a thick shock of black hair positioned himself forward. He introduced himself as Senator Richard Brent, and he thanked the Commandant for coming, as well as several other notables. He said he was proud to represent Virginia and Governor Barbour, who could not make the trip up from Richmond.

He turned over the ceremony to another man, an older man with a stentorian voice. This man gave a long and somewhat accurate account of our march and subsequent capture of Derne. My memories had jumbled much of it together, especially for the march itself, but the speaker made it seem as if we were much more heroic than I think was actually the case. As for the battle itself, that was more accurate, even if it seemed to put the lieutenant in command rather than the general.

After the account was read, letters from the governor, the lieutenant governor, and even Thomas Jefferson, were read. All praised the bravery and fortitude exhibited by their native son.

Finally, the Sword of Virginia was presented, a singular honor. It was patterned after the sword Hamet Bashaw had given him, but it looked more like a weapon of war, which seemed more befitting. It was a beautiful blade. On one side, the sword bore the inscription, "Presented by the State of Virginia to her gallant son Priestly N. O'Bannon." On the reverse side was inscribed, "Assault the conquest of the City of Derne in Africa, 27 April 1805." Underneath the eagle's head on the hilt was a gold plate depicting the lieutenant standing on the ramparts of Derne, holding in one hand the flag of the United States and in the other a sword.

Jonathan P. Brazee

I felt pride well inside of me when I saw the blade. I knew that while the sword had been presented to the lieutenant (even if his name had been misspelled), there was part of me in it as well. Part of John and Edward, too. Part of Bernard, James, Dave, and Sergeant Campbell. Part of Constantine and the rest of the Greeks. Even part of Hamet Bashaw and his troops. We had all sweated and bled for a cause.

A simple sword does not matter much in God's scheme of things. But as a symbol of how we suffered and what we accomplished despite the odds against us, I fervently hoped that it would live on, and that future Marines would remember us. What we achieved on the shores of Tripoli should never be forgotten.

Thank you for reading *From the Shores of Tripoli*. I hope you enjoyed it.

If you would like updates on new books releases, news, or special offers, please consider signing up for my mailing list. Your email will not be sold, rented, or in any other way disseminated. If you are interested, please sign up at the link below:

http://eepurl.com/bnFSHH

Other Books by Jonathan Brazee

The Return of the Marines Trilogy
The Few
The Proud
The Marines

The Al Anbar Chronicles: First Marine Expeditionary Force--Iraq
Prisoner of Fallujah
Combat Corpsman
Sniper

The United Federation Marine Corps
Recruit
Sergeant
Lieutenant
Captain
Major
Lieutenant Colonel
Colonel
Commandant

Jonathan P. Brazee

Rebel
(Set in the UFMC universe.)

Werewolf of Marines

Werewolf of Marines: Semper Lycanus
Werewolf of Marines: Patria Lycanus
Coming: Book Three

To The Shores of Tripoli

Wererat

Darwin's Quest: The Search for the Ultimate Survivor

Venus: A Paleolithic Short Story

Non-Fiction

Exercise for a Longer Life

Author Website
http://www.returnofthemarines.com

Made in the USA
Las Vegas, NV
03 July 2024

91835660R00105